The Secrets of Jedira

Cal Davis

DEDICATION

For Lydia, Attikus, Lillian, and Adonis

Reading should be fun!

ISBN: 978-1-962318-02-0

Cover by Randi Gammons

Table of Contents

Section 1

Assignment

The fifteen-year-old humanoid stood in awe. Braven Triton had just received a communiqué from the School of Discovery Scouting accepting his application.

"Mom! Dad!" he yelled.

Braven ran into their central room and found the two cleaning up a small houseplant that had been knocked onto the floor. Mom was cradling the little specimen as she was Alpha Colony's chief botanist; Dad was sweeping up the detritus and made more of a mess by scattering the cellulose.

His parents looked up. Braven gasped. He knew how important plant life was to his mother.

"Oh no. Not the brasanthum." Braven smirked. There were at least ten of the same type of plant in that room alone.

Mom gave him a don't-go-there look.

"Uh, did you get any news?" Dad redirected the

focus.

"I did!" Braven's face lit up. "I was accepted to the Scouting School." Braven was glowing with disbelief.

The Discovery Scouting program was very diverse. Potential Scouts were trained in exploration techniques, survival methods, physical endurance, technology, and discipline. Their motto was "Search, Explore, and Discover to Expand Humanoid Habitation." Braven was thrilled at the opportunity to visit strange new worlds and to have exciting adventures.

Mom caressed her fallen plant and laid it on the table. She quickly made her way to her son to congratulate him on this success. Dad threw up his arms in victory. They were so proud his dream was becoming a reality for him.

Braven had daydreamed of becoming a Discovery Scout ever since he saw the heroism in Weston, his Scout friend. He admired him and wanted to make a difference in someone else's life as Weston had done for him.

"I have to wait until my sixteenth birthday."

"So, we still have you for another three months." Mom always outwardly displayed her love for her son.

"Plenty of time for you to get prepared." Dad was always the practical one. "It's not like going to a university where you just sit all day."

"I know. This is what I want to do."

"We are proud of you, son, and we know you will

succeed in whatever you set out to do." Mom again hugged him tightly.

***

Three months passed too quickly. Braven tried to see all his friends, especially Khara Lucent. She was a close, longtime friend from Delta Colony who saved his life a couple of times. He enjoyed spending time with her. There were a few others he wished he had taken time to see, but, as usual, his visit with Khara was longer than he had planned. He would keep up with them through the N-Line Communications System.

He heard the occasional boom from the colony expansion. Since the air portal was to the north of the colony, the settlements were progressing toward the south. There were already thousands of humanoids in Alpha Colony alone. He wondered if he would ever return to the planet after the Academy. Discovery Scouts were trained for exploration. Jedira had been occupied for almost his entire life and had no more to explore.

Tomorrow was the big day. His air shuttle launched promptly at dawn, and he planned to be at the air portal in plenty of time. He sat with his parents on that final evening. Weston came for his last visit and informed him of some things to be keenly aware of as he was at the Academy. Dad and Mom encouraged him by talking about how he was such a survivor and could overcome obstacles even better than any adult they had seen. They reminded him of his past survivals and how this would be a simple event for him. He remembered the times he thought he would die from starvation or being eaten alive by a monster, but as his parents reminded him, he did survive. He tried not to dwell on those memories.

He went to his room to rest. His sleeper was comfortable, but his excitement about the upcoming events kept sleep at bay. He watched as Wilstor, Jedira's largest and brightest moon, made its way across the sky. Sometime during the night, he drifted into a peaceful rest.

***

Braven's databoard alerted him. He looked at the time and realized what the day would bring. He got up to clean and get ready for departure. He looked around his room to see if there was anything else he could not live without. He had cleaned it thoroughly and removed everything he had collected over the past years. He knew he would not return except for rare visits. Scouts were assigned to their duty stations upon graduation.

Mom and Dad were up and ready to see their son's departure. They all walked to the Lounge, the local food distribution center, for their morning meal. The air portal was located at the north edge of Alpha Colony so it would only take them a few minutes to arrive.

"Hi, Braven." Skylar, his young genius friend from

Zeta Colony, walked into the Lounge. "When are you leaving?"

"Hey, Skylar. Going to the portal in about fifteen minutes."

"Send us a message when you get there." The eleven-year-old youngster had been Braven's shadow for many years. The two had bonded during their crisis at the now-abandoned Zeta Colony. Braven knew he would hear of his little genius friend in the future when he created something to prolong life or discovered a new way to make a planet habitable.

"Oh, I will. I don't know how much I can communicate during training, but you'll hear from me."

Khara arrived next. Braven was happy to see her one last time. They chatted for a few moments and vowed to keep in contact. After last-minute goodbyes from the friends present, the Tritons made their way back to their unit and then to the air portal.

The air shuttle was the transport to the space portal, where Braven would board the space shuttle for transport to the Academy. The air shuttle was not enormous but not small. It could carry around two hundred passengers with luggage and cargo.

"Are you ready for this?" Mom had a deeply concerned expression on her face.

"I think I am, but are you?" Braven tried to ease her

a bit.

"Braven will excel," Dad stated with a look of assurance. "He has only to take the first step."

His parents had the utmost confidence in their son. Braven was proud of them and the closeness of his family. It made him feel secure when everything else was falling apart.

Braven checked in and was directed to his waiting area. His mother gave her usual motherly hug, and he had to bend for her forehead kiss. Dad gave a bear hug. They would miss him as he would them, but Braven needed to pursue his dreams. They all understood and encouraged that reality.

After boarding, Braven found his assigned seat and made himself comfortable for the trip. The window next to him faced the opposite direction from where his parents stood, but he had already said his goodbyes.

Preliminary instructions were given, and everyone buckled into their seats. The first leg of the journey was to the space portal orbiting Jedira. There, he would board a space shuttle for the extended trip to the planet of Eden, where the Academy was located.

Braven pulled out his databoard to continue reading his book by Jaulson Reddling, who explained the detailed expeditions of Discovery Scouts through the years and their contribution to humanoid civilization. Braven was proud to be selected for the Academy and was ready to start his life's adventures.

Within two hours, the air shuttle docked at the Jediran space portal. All five habitable planets had their own space portal where travelers would dock when arriving or leaving. Space shuttles were assigned specifically between two planets and were marked with the names of those two planets on the exterior of the shuttle as well as on directing signs. There was no question about which shuttle to board.

Upon departure from the air shuttle, he followed the signage for the flight to Eden. He checked in and discovered the wait would be four hours. He decided to settle in a corner to finish the book.

Compared to the other habitable planets, Eden was paradise. It was colonized by Terrans from Earth hundreds of years earlier and had become the headquarters for the Intergalactic Alliance. Most of the humanoids on Eden resembled Terrans, whereas those from Proxima B had a tougher dermis compared to the supple skin of the others. Terrans' and Edenians' skin tones ranged from very dark to very light, but none had the reddish hue of the Radzierians. Bliteque, on the other hand, was the home of the Blaukens, which were a different species of humanoid. Their skin was mauve-colored, and they had no humanoid noses. Blaukens had to wear a translator to communicate with non-

Blaukens because their vocal and hearing organs were not capable of making or hearing sounds in the intonation of other species. All symmetrical species with two arms, two legs, and one head were designated as humanoids.

Braven thought of his years living on Jedira. He was born on Eden, but his parents were assigned to Jedira when he was very young. He had lived at Alpha Colony for most of his life but had short stints at Delta and Zeta Colonies. He tried not to think of those two places and couldn't remember much about them. He stretched to the front of his window to glance at the planet he may never see again. He was excited to find out where he would go after graduation.

***

The Academy was incredible. Braven acclimated very well and made many friends. He was studious and excelled in every subject. His professors admired his hard work and exceptional grades.

Graduation Day. The day that clutched the next phase of everyone's life. This was the time to get out of training and into the "real" world. This was also when assignments were given. Braven dreamed of where he would go. Maybe to one of the new galaxies? Maybe one of the three new potentially habitable planets. What would he discover? The excitement bubbled within him.

Braven and two of his classmates had been close

friends throughout their three years at the Academy. They sat excitedly in the auditorium, awaiting the ceremony. They chatted about their potential adventures and their hopes of being assigned to the same station. At least the same planet. The physical endurance and mental challenges of the Academy prepared them for whatever they encountered. They wanted adventure, and being Discovery Scouts would provide that.

The ceremony continued. Awards were given, and finally each student's name was called for them to receive their digital certification and new assignment.

The dean called one of Braven's friends, "Clint Kosnis." He made his way to receive the items and recognition. He returned to the others and told them that he was assigned to the Pistenelle Constellation of the Borolian Quadrant. He would leave in the morning. The two friends congratulated him. That was the newest and hottest place to go.

"Spar Resits." Braven's other friend started toward the dean. He returned and shared with them. It was the same location. The two were thrilled with the assignments, and they knew Braven would join them.

"Braven Triton." Braven's heart skipped a beat. He let out a breath. He was excited, but the unknown destination took his breath. He rose and approached the dean. He received several accolades, words of congratulations, and encouragement. He started to return to his seat.

Braven opened his databoard to see his assignment. He stopped midstride on his way back to his seat and stared at his databoard. After a few moments, he realized he needed to keep moving. He met his excited friends with an "I can't believe this."

"Where are you going?" Their eyes were filled with excitement.

Braven showed them the databoard. They examined the text and then looked at their friend with confused looks.

Jedira.

Section 2

Mission

Braven waited until he got back to his room to notify his parents. Since they were on another planet, they could only view the ceremony through the Academy's N-View. He waited for an hour after he returned to his room to contact them personally.

He N-Lined his parents. He could imagine their joyful cheering in the background after he told them of his assignment. He was not as jubilant.

"This is so exciting!" Mom messaged. Dad added a cheer to the N-Line.

"Yeah." Braven hesitated for a moment. He forced a sidewards smile. "I may need my old room back." He knew that Discovery Scouts had their own living quarters, but he tried to make light of the situation.

Braven ended the N-Line with his parents. He was anxious to see them, but his dream was to search, conquer, and explore the universe. How could he do that on the same planet where he grew up? His best friends would be going to a new area for exploration. Why did he get stuck back on Jedira?

He sat back in his chair and looked at the ceiling. Closing his eyes, he thought it could be worse.

Braven, Clint, and Spar spent their last night together, talking over the last three years. The two were excited about their upcoming adventure; Braven was a little jealous and wished he could have been assigned with them or anywhere else besides the same place where he grew up. They finally surrendered to rest.

Their databoard alarms erupted simultaneously. They all finished packing their belongings and moved toward the air portal to board the air shuttle. Upon arriving at the space portal, they dispersed toward their assigned flights. Braven saw his friends off as they boarded their space shuttle to their destination. He felt disheartened as he saw the last of his buddies enter their shuttles.

Braven's space shuttle was scheduled to leave in six hours. He found a corner to get his mind settled. He had not spoken to Weston recently but knew he was still on planet so he would be able to work with him. That would be a consolation, along with being around his parents. He thought of contacting his friend. From the space shuttle, Braven could connect to the N-View link for other planets.

"You won't believe where I've been assigned,"

Braven started after their usual greetings.

"The Borolian Quadrant?" Weston excitedly guessed.

"Oh, don't get me started."

"What? I hear there are a lot of Scouts heading that way. There is a new moon that is ripe for exploration."

"Well, everyone but you-know-who gets to go there." Braven felt his words were sour.

"Where are you assigned?"

"I am coming back to Jedira."

"What! That's incredible! I heard we were getting one Scout from the Academy but never even thought of you!"

"Thanks a lot. You're not still supplying a mining camp, are you?"

Weston grimaced. "No, not anymore." He laughed.

Their conversation continued. Weston filled him in on some of his current responsibilities.

Braven's flight was on perfect schedule. His space shuttle arrived at the Jediran space station without any trouble. He boarded the air shuttle and settled in his seat for an uneventful trip home.

The trip was seemingly over by the time Braven got settled. A local Scout was waiting for him at the air portal as expected. His parents met him as well.

The Scout showed him to his new unit at the Scout camp. He was instructed to be at in-processing at first light.

Weston arrived to greet him and said that he would make sure he got there.

The Tritons, Weston, and his wife, Mesilia spent most of the evening catching up and sharing events they had already shared on the N-Line. Just a happy family reunion. He contacted Khara before retiring for the night.

The next morning, Braven reported for in-processing. He was given multiple tests and was told that since he had lived on planet before, he did not need any inoculations. Braven was relieved. He was issued standard uniforms and was informed of the Scouting way of life on Jedira.

Finally, he reported to the Scout Director, Mishel Fortuna. Director Fortuna gave him the expected welcome and introduction to the unit. He explained his chain of command and introduced Braven to one of his supervisors, Weston Hastern. Braven grinned.

"I hear you two know each other."

"Yes, sir." Braven controlled a smile. He thought about how the director had no idea how well they knew each other.

The director then scheduled him for a return appointment to see him in two days. Until then, he would be given tasks around the camp and Alpha Colony. The tasks began immediately.

Within a few minutes, Braven found himself riding

with Scout Yaltis, a seasoned Scout, in a small rover on the outskirts of the colony. Alpha Colony was the headquarters colony for the planet. There were three other active colonies scattered no more than one thousand kilometers from Alpha: Gamma, Iota, and Kappa. Delta and Zeta Colonies no longer existed. He did not know why they used names like those for colonies; he would have named them something more attractive. He had heard the names came from Earth's history, so he surmised that they were the names of some of their large cities or world leaders.

The day continued with little excitement. Scout Yaltis shared some things about Jedira until Braven shared that he had grown up on planet. He then asked Braven about the planet. Braven felt proud that he knew things someone else did not and was interested in knowing. Scout Yaltis shared that he was raised on Earth and joined the Scouts eighteen years ago. He had not returned since joining but missed his home planet and would return some day. Since it was the "mother planet," not many Scouts were assigned there.

The first two days in his new position went by quickly. He visited with Weston and was able to see his parents. He reconnected with Khara. He made new friends with the other Scouts. There were thirty other Scouts stationed there. He was not sure of their responsibilities. All of them seemed happy to have him there. He was glad and felt accepted.

Weston lived with his bride, Mesilia, in their unit at the edge of the Scout colony. Braven thought they were such a great couple and visited them after his second duty day. Mesilia was as beautiful as ever. Her skin was more radiant than he remembered.

"I didn't know there were so many Scouts on planet. I just remember you and that humanoid who went to prison." Braven remembered how the other Scout tried to have him and Weston killed.

"Right. You mean Frey. After that whole episode with Zeta Colony, I rejoined the Scouts here at Alpha. Frey will probably spend the rest of his life in the Radzierian moon prison."

"I hear that's a rough place." Braven reflected on how he and Weston were treated by him and thought that was where that humanoid male belonged.

"Yes, not much good there." Weston thought for a moment. "Within the last year, the number of Scouts increased by twelve, but six more arrived in the last two months. You were the last."

"Why are they increasing the number? Are they wanting to search the rest of the planet?"

"Not sure. I'm not in a high enough rank to know stuff like that." Weston chuckled.

On his third day, Braven arrived at Director

Fortuna's office for his scheduled meeting. There were two other Scout officials present. They welcomed the young Scout, and all sat around a small table for their discussion. Braven was oblivious as to what would happen.

Small talk began. They asked Braven about his Academy education and how well he had settled into the colony. One brought up Braven's past at both Delta and Zeta Colonies. Braven looked at the floor.

"We know these experiences had a traumatic effect on you, and we believe they have made you stronger than the average Jediran."

Braven said nothing. He wondered how he could be stronger when he almost lost his life and mind from the trauma. He sat quietly.

"Scout Triton." One of the officials closed his databoard. "We are happy you are with us. We have reviewed your case concerning these traumatic events during your childhood. We have also followed your recovery and your instruction at the Academy."

"Sir?" Braven hesitated but didn't know how to proceed.

"Will you briefly tell us about your past experiences on Jedira?"

Braven didn't like to dwell on the negative feelings of his past. He inhaled deeply and began to explain his plight as a twelve-year-old struggling with friends to survive abandonment at Delta and his encounters at Zeta Colony. He felt disturbed by even recalling the details involved.

"Your history of survival has been amazing. We commend you for your tenacity and leadership," Director Fortuna inserted.

"Thank you, but I just had to survive and protect those with me."

"That's our point. You are a survivor and protector. We see it in your resume as well as the references we received from those who knew of your encounters. You excel as a team member. You excelled at the Academy. We specifically requested your assignment to Jedira."

Braven raised his head and stared at the leader. He was embarrassed and didn't know how to respond.

"Your academic records are in the upper ten percent. There are multiple praises from your instructors and mentors."

Braven looked down and sat quietly.

"We have a mission that we are assigning to you. This will need strategy techniques and an investigating eye that sees things the way you do."

Braven didn't know he had an "investigating eye" or that he used strategy any differently than anyone else. He was a little baffled.

"Tomorrow morning, we will meet with you and the Team that you will be joining and will give you the information and directives you will need," Director Fortuna informed him and asked if he had any questions.

Braven sat quietly for a moment. "No, sir."

"Then you are dismissed. We will see you in the conference room tomorrow at zero eight hundred sharp."

"Yes, sir. Thank you, sir." Braven rose and departed the office. The three officials remained in their chairs.

His first assignment! Braven was not sure why they were meeting with him and why they had his history, but he was excited to be on a mission.

He found Weston and informed him of the mission.

"That's great!" Weston responded. "Only here three days and gets an assignment. No details, huh? It may be confidential. You may not want to talk to anyone about it."

Braven had not thought of that or the possible importance of the mission. He did not want to compromise it in any way. He thought Weston was such a wise man. He was glad to be serving with him.

Braven returned to his unit and thought about his old pals from the Academy. He had sent an earlier message and checked the N-Line for a response. Spar and Clint were roommates on a potentially habitable moon surrounding the giant gas planet B16RM2S in the Borolian Quadrant. They had already gone on a mission and loved being there. Braven felt a bit of jealousy arise. He wanted so much to be there. He returned a message but didn't mention his upcoming mission, and then rested for the night.

***

Braven met Weston at the Lounge for breakfast. They discussed nothing of importance. Braven saw that he would need to leave in a few minutes, so he told his friend he was leaving.

"I'll walk with you."

Braven was glad he could do that. He wasn't sure of where Weston's duty was that day, but he knew the seasoned Scout had it under control.

As they arrived at the conference room, Weston walked in with his young friend. Braven wondered when he would be leaving for his duty.

"Let's sit over here."

"Are you on this mission, too?"

"I have been all along." Weston grinned. "I didn't want to spoil your surprise."

"You are not right." Braven gave him a smile.

"Oh, you just say it because it's true." The two chuckled.

Director Fortuna and the two officials entered the room of twelve Scouts. They took their seats behind the front table and waited for everyone to get settled.

"I see everyone is present. Welcome to Scout Braven Triton on his first assignment out of the Academy." The director smiled as if he was pleased to see him.

The group welcomed Braven.

"Here are the details of Mission Groundbreak. We are moving a ground attachment toward the south. This is away from the equator; therefore, it may be cooler than you are accustomed to here at Alpha. You will be provided with environmental protection gear. Preliminary reports show that some types of anomalies have become widespread in the area and are moving. These anomalies specifically include seismic activity. We are not sure what this is. Scouts Mezlin and Archer have taken the hilo to survey the area, but nothing has been verified.

"Our mission is to search out the causes of these events. Take samples, digiphotos, and atmospheric and seismic readings. We need to know what is going on."

"Sir, if this is only seismic activity, why do you need to investigate it?" one of the Scouts inquired with a puzzled look on his face.

"Good question. Because it is moving toward Alpha Colony."

There was a low rumble of whispers.

"What do you mean, 'it's moving toward Alpha'?"

"Exactly what I said. Something is causing seismic activity to move in one direction."

"Something?"

"Something could mean an underground volcano as far as we know right now. This has never been encountered on any planet before now, and we are not waiting around for something to happen on this one.

"Satellite images, schematics, and digiphotos of the area are included in the secure message you are receiving now." One of the officials sent data from her databoard. "If you look closely, there are land formations unlike any around here. Some of these are impassable. The hilos will deliver the Team across the chasms.

"We have projected that with the consistent movement and velocity, the anomaly will be at the first chasm within sixty days. You will need to get your information and return to camp before that happens. We are not sure of what would happen if a humanoid remained there when it arrives."

"It?"

Silence.

"You will depart at noon today. Get your personal business in order," Director Fortuna offered, or warned, the group before dismissing.

Braven was still a bit confused, so he asked Weston on the way out of the room.

"What does he mean to get our personal business in order?"

"He always ends with that statement because any mission can be dangerous. We are not promised that we will return from any of them."

"Can I see my parents?"

"As long as you are back in time to leave."

"Got it."

Braven hurried back to his unit to get his belongings ready, then went by the supply station to pick up any gear assigned to him. After packing his backpack, he took a shuttle into Alpha Colony to visit his parents, then returned in plenty of time to be the first at the departure depot.

He pondered the mission and the information he was given. He reviewed the message filled with documents, digiphotos, and maps. He wondered about the director's words in referring to "it" and "something" as if there were some creature causing seismic quakes. He doubted there were creatures on any planet large enough to do that.

He sat at the departure depot when Weston arrived. The hilo was being readied, and the other Scouts soon arrived. Within minutes, they boarded and lifted into the air.

The hilo rose above the colony and circled around toward the south. Braven had never traveled that direction. The local terrain was the usual low-lying, cyan-colored vegetation on flat land with the occasional monoliths jutting up randomly in groups.

He talked with Weston through an individual channel on his headset. Weston and Mesilia were expecting a little one in a few months. He was so excited to be a father. Mesilia would be an amazing mother. Her Blauken motherliness would smother the child in love. Braven wondered who the baby would resemble dark-brown skin from Weston or Mesilia's beautiful mauve skin. Would the child have a nose or need to wear a translator? Either way, he knew the baby would be surrounded by family love. And Braven's family would add to the affection.

The landscape changed the farther south the hilo traveled. After about six hundred kilometers, they crossed the chasms. Braven noticed that numerous monoliths popped up in larger assemblages. The monoliths were straight, vertical, granite-like rock structures that were erected out of the ground with no sense of a pattern. Each of the structures was topped with mesas. Nothing grew on the flat tops. When a group of monoliths were close to each other, flora grew abundantly inside the grouping as well as down the sides of the structures.

Scout Mezlin interrupted over the headsets letting them know to be ready to disembark. The hilo circled until the pilot found a large open area where she gently let the aircraft come to rest. The group exited the vessel.

"We will make base camp here and begin our investigation in the morning."

Capria, Jedira's star, was close to setting. Camp was set up, a perimeter was established, and lights were erected. Braven enjoyed watching everyone work as a team, as they all had their own duties to perform. His job was to erect the lights around the perimeter. He paced off where to set the next. As he was setting the base, he recalled how the lights kept him safe at Zeta Colony. *Maybe I should put the lights closer together,* he thought.

He had two lights left to erect when another Scout came to him. "You finish this one, and I'll get the last one."

"Thanks." Braven started on his last one. He enjoyed the teamwork that seemed second nature to the Scouts.

A central table was set up for meetings. Everyone gathered to discuss the next day's plans. Braven was one of the Scouts assigned to digiphotos.

After a meal of rations, the Scouts sat and talked for a few hours. Soon, one by one, they retired to their sleepers. Two-hour shifts were given to four Scouts on a one-man watch schedule.

Section 3

Remembrance

Braven opened his eyes to Capria's early dawn. The stillness in the air was alluring. He got ready to face the day. A few other Scouts meandered about the camp.

Braven had been assigned to meal duty, so he accessed the food storage container and retrieved breakfast meals for everyone. He placed the meals and drinks on the camp table and annotated the items on the inventory list.

Within the hour, Capria was peeking over the horizon, and Scouts were busy getting ready for the day's duties. Scout Archer, the mission director, announced that they would be departing in fifteen minutes.

Braven took one of the Digital Photographic Imagers to become more familiar with it before they began their exploration. The image-takers had all been given preliminary instructions, but he could tell there were many features that were not explained. He pushed a button to reveal former digiphotos. He reviewed them and knew that those should have been downloaded before this mission. He asked Weston for help. The older Scout showed him an input port on a mainframe in the hilo. He helped Braven clear out the data storage.

Braven was ready to be his team's digiphoto expert. He took several shots around the camp interior and of some of the Scouts. Many threw up their hands, but the "expert" caught their morning faces anyway. He captured shots of the cyan flora outside camp in Capria's morning light. Braven enjoyed his task.

The group gathered for a morning hike of two kilometers to get closer to the epicenter of the disturbances. Scout Archer led the formation as each Scout carried his own necessary equipment for the day. A small MiniRover was disconnected from the hilo to carry heavier supplies and equipment so the Scouts would not expend their strength carrying the extra weight. The pilot remained at the camp with the hilo in case of emergencies, and her responsibility was to gather input from the Teams to compile a database for review and to coordinate locations and communication.

Braven took digiphotos of every new landscape they came upon. The number of monoliths increased immensely as they continued toward their destination.

A somewhat familiar odor penetrated his senses. Braven knew he had experienced that smell before, but it was too far back in his mind. One of the Scouts asked about the odd smell, but only Braven remembered it from somewhere. Comments were made, but there were no conclusions.

The director announced to set up the operations camp. He contacted Scout Mezlin at base camp to establish their bivouac location. Within minutes, Scouts were paired and departed in various directions. Open lines of communication were required for the safety of all Scouts. Air drones were released to scour the area ahead of the teams and for reconnaissance.

Braven was paired with Scout Timlo Estavines. He was a two-year Scout, had been on Jedira for the last month, and was very quiet. Braven had not even spoken with him until that day. He had only heard him say "yes, sir" once.

The two headed toward the south with another pair. After one-half kilometer, they parted ways. Braven and Timlo made it to the side of a deep depression in the landscape. A sudden drop in topography made the more seasoned Scout nervous so he backed away a few steps.

"Afraid of heights?"

"Uh-huh."

At least he does communicate, Braven thought.

Braven pulled out the imager and captured digiphotos of the surrounding area. Timlo, assigned to seismology, placed sensors in the ground along the edge of the depression. They moved along the rim as Braven made digiphotos of numerous landforms and monoliths. The terrain was very different, and he captured some interesting scenery. The depressions looked as though that section of land had caved in. Some of the depressions were elongated while others were circular.

Timlo planted seismic detectors along the ridge. The two surveyed the topography and made measurements between the various formations. They scanned the area for any life but, as expected, nothing was around. There had been only one recorded life source on the planet, other than humanoids and flora. He recalled that the exception was a caprodome from years ago, and he prayed there were no more of those creatures.

Suddenly, the pair felt vibrations under their feet. They froze and looked at their surroundings. The tremblors stopped as quickly as they began.

Timlo grunted and resumed placing sensors. Braven was curious if it was over and if it would happen again anytime soon. He peered around and continued with his image-capturing.

At midday, the pair rested with their lunch. Braven discussed plans for the afternoon; Timlo grunted in agreement.

"So, where is your home?" Braven tried to get to

know his companion.

After a short delay, the response came. "Proxima B."

"You have any family?"

After a short pause, he answered, "No."

Silence.

"What about those quakes? I don't remember them ever happening on planet."

No reply. Braven's companion continued dining. He could see he was not making much headway with his fellow Scout, so he decided to let it rest.

They continued their afternoon duties after their short break and soon word came to wrap it up and return to the operations camp. They gathered their belongings and started back.

Upon their arrival, they saw other Scouts had already returned. Each team downloaded their findings into the MiniRover which was uploaded to the database in the hilo and then to the central database at the Scout camp at Alpha. Braven and Timlo uploaded their day's data and found a place to sit with the others.

When all teams arrived, they struck out for their base camp for the night. The two-kilometer hike was over before Braven realized. He had enjoyed his first "real" day on the job. He delivered his backpack to his sleeper and joined the group for the team meeting.

Scout Archer asked for a debrief. Each team detailed

their findings. Braven presented for his team. He mentioned the small tremblor, but no one else felt it. One thing that was consistent was the numerous monoliths in every direction more than anyone had ever seen.

After the debriefing, Braven set out the evening rations and marked the inventory.

Braven took a seat by Weston. He noticed Timlo was sitting by himself. He wondered if his partner would ever be open enough to talk to anyone.

As the evening closed, the Scouts turned in for a night's rest.

***

On the third day of their mission, Capria peeked over the horizon. The past two days were not memorable since nothing out of the ordinary was experienced. They prepared for another day. Braven laid out breakfast and set out the prepared midday meal kits.

The group struck out toward the west-southwest, and teams split off at intervals. Braven and his silent teammate followed their assigned directions toward the west for one kilometer and then south for one-half.

Braven sniffed that same odd odor as before. The smell grew stronger and began to encompass them the farther they hiked. It gripped his mind like he should know where he had encountered it before.

As they walked, Timlo finally spoke. "What is that

odor?"

His words startled Braven as he was not expecting to hear any vocals during their trips.

"Uh..." Braven gathered his thoughts. "I don't know. I smelled it before but not sure what it was."

They approached a large chasm. It was impassable. It looked about two kilometers across and hundreds of kilometers to the right and left. The two scoured the area for anything of interest. Inside the abyss, large conical spears reached kilometers high. Vapor could be seen rising from the chasm floor. The stench had greatly increased to the point that the two covered their noses.

Braven made digiphotos of everything inside and around the chasm. Timlo placed two sensors and backed away from the gorge. Braven followed him. The reeking odor made his stomach nauseous, and he vomited. The pair gathered their equipment and quickly moved a long distance away before stopping to surmise the situation.

Braven puked again.

"That must be the worst odor I have ever smelled."

Timlo grunted in agreement. He wiped liquid from his eyes.

"I think we should move away from here and let Scout Archer know about it," Braven suggested.

Another sound of agreement.

They retraced their steps for one kilometer and

contacted Scout Archer.

"Yes, sir. It is pretty vile. The odor is overwhelming. It seems to be emanating from the chasm. Something here is not right." Braven couldn't think of the correct words to explain.

"Triton, what do you mean 'not right'?"

"I think you may need to see this for yourself, sir."

At about that time, another team reported to Scout Archer the same events. They had hiked with Braven and Timlo but split off heading south one-half kilometer before Braven's team. They must have had the same experience.

Scout Archer asked the two teams to do surveillance away from that area, and they would discuss it at the briefing tonight. Braven was glad he was able to capture some of the images of the area before he had to leave. They may help in understanding what was there.

The team found another area to survey. Sensors were set, and digiphotos were taken. They were relieved when the call to return to base camp was made.

Braven and Timlo were the first to arrive at the operations camp. They began uploading their data to the MiniRover. Before long, other teams arrived and asked what they found. Braven tried to explain how he felt.

"It was the worst odor I've ever smelled!"

"He threw up," Timlo announced matter-of-factly.

Everyone gasped and couldn't respond.

Timlo grinned.

The whole group erupted in laughter.

Through Braven's chuckles, he had to ask his friend, "So, that's the first thing you can say?"

Timlo smiled.

Finally, the last team arrived, and the group headed back to base camp.

Braven set out the evening victuals.

Scout Archer began the briefing. The two teams had the same story. Overpowering odor. Deep, spiney chasm. Neither team could remain at the scene for very long. After the reports were concluded, the mission director dismissed the meeting.

"Scouts Hastern and Triton, I want to speak with you both."

After the other Scouts left, the pair approached the leader.

"Do either of you have any remembrance of the odor you encountered in the past two days?"

Weston and Braven looked at each other. They both looked puzzled.

"Does this odor remind you of Zeta Colony?"

Braven stared at the mission director. His mind searched for an answer. In the deep thoughts of yesteryear, Braven's mind wandered over his short time at Zeta. He remembered that the smell at the colony was somewhat similar. He felt something more was there that he could not remember. He thought of the walks he had. He remembered he met Weston there. And Skylar. They weren't there for long when the colony was evacuated. There was another place, Braven contemplated, where the odor was stronger than at the colony.

He looked at Weston whose eyes were fixed on him. Braven frowned then a rush of anxiety flooded him. The mining camp! He had suppressed the odor that was so prevalent at Zeta Colony and, he later discovered, was present when the monster was nearby. He suddenly remembered how the odor reminded him of danger.

Braven's eyes widened. He froze. He couldn't breathe. He couldn't think. His body trembled. A volcano of hidden internal debilities erupted. He gasped.

Weston put his arm around Braven's shoulders and reminded him of the Scout Guide's instructions for when danger was close. He calmly spoke to his friend. "You are in a safe place. We surround you. Nothing will harm you."

Braven looked at Weston and then at Scout Archer. "I can't do this." Tears welled up in his eyes. His breathing returned with a vengeance.

"Braven." The calming voice that he knew so well enveloped his being.

Braven's hyperventilation slightly slowed. He took a deep, staggered breath and released it slowly through his nose. He wiped the moisture off his cheek. He found a chair to avoid falling.

"I'm sorry, Scout Archer." He could barely speak.

"Scout Triton, I am told you are a brave young man. I've read your bio and know you have been through much danger. Director Fortuna instructed me how you may react as you have."

Braven swallowed hard. He wanted that part of his life forever gone, along with all the memories of it.

"You're going to be okay." Weston patted Braven's shoulder.

"Sometimes I wonder," Braven finally whispered.

"Scout Triton, you were selected for this mission because you have more personal information than any other humanoid about the events we are going to encounter. I need you to be mentally strong and use your expertise when the time comes. Protect your fellow Scouts and the inhabitants of this planet. Scout Hastern is familiar with the events at Zeta as well and will be your support."

Braven was glad Weston was present, but he wanted to get off planet.

"Tomorrow will be a different mission for you. Get some rest, and I will brief you at daybreak." At that, the mission director left the two alone.

"What is he talking about? What expertise do I have? I was almost eaten."

"When the time comes, you'll know."

Braven groaned. "I hate it when people say that."

Section 4

Revelation

Braven couldn't sleep. The odor lingered in his nostrils and plagued his mind. He stared out the top window of his sleeper at the starry sky.

What if there were more caprodomes? Fear trickled through his body. He scanned the dark sky for any signs of movement. Wilstor was shining brightly, so that would keep those creatures at bay. There was also the perimeter fencing. Even though he resolved he was safe, his internal senses were on high alert.

Time passed, and he knew he needed rest. He opened his databoard to check his personal messages. Nothing. He reviewed his current mission docs. Boring. He thought of other topics to distract his mind from past dangers, but visions kept plaguing him.

He sat up. He had to overcome this. He exited his sleeper to a quiet, dark world. The only lights available were along the perimeter and from Wilstor's quickly disappearing light. He walked toward the perimeter. The three-meter-tall fence protected the camp, not just with the light, but with the power field that surged through each rod. If anything tried to enter, an energy blast would make it immobile. This type of protection had not occurred to Braven, but there was no fauna on Jedira except for the one caprodome that had been removed from the planet, so why would this protection be needed. No other creatures had been discovered. *But was there only one caprodome?* Braven shuddered.

"Couldn't sleep?"

Braven was startled. He turned his head toward the voice. Scout Able. He couldn't remember his last name. He didn't know him very well since he had not worked closely with him.

"Um, no. Too much going through my mind, I guess."

Scout Able found an open chair and claimed it as his own. Braven did the same.

"Where is your home planet?"

"Born on Eden but raised here." Braven thought about his being raised on Jedira. He remembered his birth planet, Eden, but his family was reassigned when he was very young. Jedira was starkly different from Eden where lush greenery of all shapes, sizes, and colors flourished and multiple species of fauna thrived.

"From here?"

Braven grunted affirmatively. "You?"

"I'm Terran."

"I hear there are a lot of humanoids on Earth."

"Around twelve billion."

Braven gasped and frowned at his colleague. Braven could not imagine that many humanoids were on one planet.

"That's why the government started the colonization program. Earth couldn't handle much more growth, so they shipped hundreds of millions of Terrans to Eden and then to Proxima B. Every new planet gets a supply."

"My ancestors are from Earth, but I don't know how many generations ago. I've never been there."

"It's a nice planet. Much more beautiful than here, but there are so many people, and that causes too many restrictions. We couldn't travel outside our jurisdiction without permission. We had limitations on the size of our home, the size of any meetings, even the amount of food we kept at one time. I like being with the Intergalactic Alliance and in the Scouting program. So much more liberty."

"Sounds like it," Braven could not imagine living in those restrictions. "How long have you been on Jedira?"

"I have been here a few years."

The two continued meaningless talk until Scout Able mentioned Capria was rising. Braven sighed. He had not been able to sleep at all, and now he would have a full day ahead of him.

Braven readied himself for the day and then hurried to get the morning and midday meals arranged.

Scout Archer announced that he wanted a meeting before anyone left for their duties. As the group gathered, Braven anticipated how the day's duties would change.

"Morning, Scouts."

A rumble of return greetings was heard.

"We will be changing our focus a bit today. Yesterday, two teams found very interesting evidence at the epicenter of our investigation. We will be searching from above while everyone grounded will conduct a physical search. We will focus on less area. Assignments were uploaded to your databoards." They were dismissed.

Braven opened his databoard. Air search. *What does that mean?*

"Weston, what does this mean?"

"You're with me in the air today. We will be investigating from the sky."

Braven hesitated. "Is that good? I guess I'm confused."

"You'll see."

Braven grabbed his gear and joined Weston as he headed toward the hilo. Upon arrival, he noticed another Scout already inside. Timlo. *Timlo? Why was Timlo on this mission? He was afraid of heights.*

As the hilo lifted, Braven examined his quiet teammate. Late twenties, light complexion with dark hair. Typical-looking humanoid male from his planet. He wondered why Timlo was so quiet; not that quietness was a negative sign, but it was unusual in such a close group. He had been stationed on the planet for a month and should have gotten to know others by now. Such a mystery but Braven wasn't that interested in humanoid psychology.

As they hovered over the towers, Braven took multiple images of the tops and sides of the monoliths all the way to the horizon. The stone towers thickly dotted the landscape.

"Why are there so many monoliths here rather than to the north near Alpha?"

No response.

"What caused these anyway? Geologic tectonics do not cause these."

Braven was curious but, again, no response.

"Scouts, this is your mission. What are these? How are they created? And do they pose a threat to humanoid life on this planet? Take us down," Scout Archer ordered the pilot. The hilo slowly descended and hovered at the top of one of the monoliths.

"Scout Estavines, Scout Triton. Take some samples."

Braven looked at Timlo. How would he react to this order?

Without hesitation, Timlo grabbed the specimen kit and reached for his straps. Braven followed his lead.

The two Scouts harnessed up and rappelled to the top of the monoliths six meters below. The barren top had appeared from above to be dirt, but upon touching the surface, they discovered it was soft and spongy. The Scouts quickly took specimens from the surface. Braven made some images, and then they alerted the pilot to bring them up.

As the hilo lifted and moved to another location, the pair quickly uploaded their specimens and readied themselves for four more descents. All went as planned. During some of their rappelling, the hilo maneuvered to the sides of the monoliths to get specimens from flora attached. Not every tower had flora attached.

The hilo circled the area and headed back to camp.

It was just after midday when they arrived at camp. Braven and Timlo discussed analyzing the data they had collected.

Upon landing, Braven grabbed his gear and got off the hilo with a small leap to the ground. He felt something hit his foot. He looked around the ground, but nothing was out of the ordinary, so he started toward the center table to begin his assessment. After a few steps, he felt like he had stepped in a hole with his other foot. He stopped to examine his boot.

There was a large hole in the front of the sole, and the rest of the sole was deteriorated. Braven quickly removed his left boot to examine. He examined the other to find the same.

"Uh, someone, something is wrong. Scout Archer? Weston?"

Scout Archer looked at the young Scout to see his damaged footwear. He hurried to Braven as did Weston.

"Scout Archer?" Timlo spoke. He held up his footwear.

"What happened? You two must have picked up something from the towers?"

"Must have." Braven removed his sock, which came off in two pieces. The bottom of his foot had red splotches.

"Scout Hastern, get the med kit," Scout Archer directed.

The two Scouts moved to the central table to sit, their footwear and socks were removed. The bottoms of their feet had blistered.

"Any pain?"

Negative replies.

Weston gave them sanitary wipes. The two cleaned their feet thoroughly.

"Take a sample of what's on the shoes for analysis. Evidently, you picked that up on top of the monoliths. Didn't you say the surface was spongy?"

"Yes, sir," Braven answered.

"There may be more to these rock towers than we have seen before."

Was it the tops of the monoliths or just something that was picked up? Why were the tower tops spongy? That was not a typical rock surface. Maybe some flora was underneath the dirt which made it feel that way. Braven couldn't imagine what caused his shoes to disintegrate as quickly as they did.

"We'll get you two some more footwear. Our investigation may have turned just a bit." Scout Archer instructed Scout Mezlin to contact HQ to send footwear replacements as well as a few extra supplies. He also asked her to send back physical data samples for analysis.

Braven sat quietly with Timlo at the central table with their bare feet propped up. They reviewed their databoard information. In the four days of the mission, Braven had taken hundreds, possibly thousands, of images. He began the process of organizing them into similar groupings.

It was late afternoon, and the other Scout teams finally returned.

"Well, let's just take it easy after a long hilo-ride," came one humorous comment.

"Teacher's Pet!"

Braven countered with a big smile and shrug.

After the returning Scouts saw the damaged shoes and the blistered feet, they had more sympathy.

Scout Able was the assigned medic, and he examined their feet. He instructed and helped them to flush thoroughly with water in hopes of removing anything causing the blisters and avoiding more damage to the skin.

Meal duty was reassigned to another Scout who brought the injured Scouts their evening meals. Braven's and Timlo's injuries increased during the afternoon, and they could not walk due to the blisters. A couple of Scouts carried them to their sleepers.

Braven lay for hours trying to get some sleep. His feet were burning. He stared through the top screen at the dots of light. He wondered how much excitement his friends were having in the Borolian Quadrant. He wished he could have joined them. Maybe someday he could be reassigned.

The stars blinked as if something momentarily shaded them from his view. Braven opened his eyes wide.

Could it be? He stared more intently to see any other unusual motions in the night sky. Nothing.

Memories flooded Braven's mind. He caught his increased breathing and purposefully slowed it. He used techniques his counselor had taught him to rid his mind of terrifying memories. He pulled his blanket closer to his chin and stared into the dark. The unmoving starry lights drowned him in heaviness. Very soon, his eyes were heavy, and sleep overtook him.

***

The next morning, Braven awoke with terrible burning on his feet. He saw that the skin on the bottom of his feet had broken and oozed blood during the night. He slid to the opening in his sleeper and called for someone. Weston heard his call, and when he saw the blood, he called Scout Able and retrieved the med kit.

After examining Braven's feet, the medic washed them thoroughly and then applied antibacterial spray and steroid cream. He didn't know how to treat these injuries because he didn't know what had caused them. Medic duties were assigned in rotation since Scouts learned basic medicine at the Academy. Also, they had limited medical supplies at the bivouac.

Braven told Weston about the night sighting. Weston said he should notify Scout Archer today after the teams leave.

Braven and Timlo were carried to the central tables where they could sit with their feet elevated and be a part of the group meeting. He was glad to be a part of a group that cared for each other the way they all did.

Scout Archer addressed the group.

"Scouts, it appears that there is more to the monoliths than we anticipated. Scouts Estavines and Triton encountered something on the tops of the towers that caused physical injuries. I want to refocus our investigation on the towers. Are they truly rock towers as we have always assumed? Does something live on or inside them that we need to know about? I want answers." At that, he dismissed the teams for their new assignments.

The injured Scouts remained at camp and were instructed to review their data. Braven informed Scout Archer of the possible sightings he had had the night before. He was asked to log his sightings into the database for future reference.

Braven inspected his digiphotos. One after another, he scrolled through the daily folders: images of his fellow Scouts, the hilo, the MiniRover, the monoliths, the dotted landscape, flora, and the sky. He reviewed some of the ones he had captured on top of the towers. He zoomed in to see if there were any types of flora or movement. Nothing.

After a few hours, a hilo arrived with the necessary medicine and supplies for the camp. There was new footwear for the two Scouts, but they were unable to try them on. Medicine was administered to their feet and quickly began the soothing restoration.

"Timlo," Braven said as he took a break from his databoard, "I thought you were afraid of heights."

Timlo just looked at his fellow Scout.

"You didn't even hesitate to jump out of the hilo at

six meters above ground."

Timlo lowered his head. "It was an order."

Braven stared at the Scout. He was inspired by his loyalty. *Could I have done that? He overcame his fear to fulfill an order.*

"Would you obey every order given to you?"

"Of course. Our superiors have the experience to know and to conduct the most logical approach. It was our duty to take samples, and we were instructed to do it."

"You never disobey an order?"

A look of confusion settled on Timlo's face. "Why? I trust my superiors to do what is right. I joined to be a Scout. If we disobey orders, what kind of team would we be?"

Braven thought. "We wouldn't be a team."

"Exactly. I love being a Scout. It's a high honor to be in this group. Why would I want to destroy the unity and comradery with my team members or not be trusted by my superiors?"

Braven's mind swirled at Timlo's elevated loyalty. He had never seen anyone with this mindset. He admired his fellow Scout and hoped he could be like him someday.

It became quiet again as the pair examined their data. That was the most he had heard Timlo speak since he had known him.

Image after image, tower after tower, image after

image, tower after tower. It never stopped. After hours of trudging through the data, Braven's eyes were tired. He rubbed his hands over his face and through his hair.

"Timlo, it's the same images day after day. I think I need to delete some of these so I can narrow down my search."

"Well, closely compare each one before you delete anything."

"I just need to focus somewhere and don't know where to start."

"Start at the beginning."

"Really?" Braven raised his eyebrow sarcastically.

"Compare one image from early in the mission to another of the same location taken later."

Why hadn't I thought of that? He is so logical.

Dozens of the images were taken from various locations and angles throughout the last six days. He opened his first day's folder and searched for the initial images from after their arrival. He went to the final day in the field before their hilo mission. He found pairs of images taken on their hike at the exact same place from almost the same angle but four days apart. He had taken so many images that he didn't even remember making those, but the date/time stamp was present. He matched hundreds of these pairs, and then he stopped and looked intently at two images.

"What's this?" He put the two images side-by-side. He used the layover tool so he could see one through the other.

"Found it!" Braven was astounded yet puzzled. "Timlo, look at this."

The Scout leaned over to look at Braven's databoard. Braven explained the layout and the two dates. On day four, a tower appeared in the background that was not present on day one.

"How can these towers just appear like that?"

The Scouts were extremely baffled.

Timlo looked back at his databoard. "What are those coordinates?"

Braven gave him the exact location. Timlo scrolled through his databoard. He stopped and closely analyzed some data.

"There was seismic activity at that exact location on day two of our mission."

"So, what does that mean?"

"Maybe the seismic activity is caused by the growth of these towers."

"How can these rock towers grow so quickly?"

After a short pause, Timlo responded. "Maybe they are not rock."

Section 5

New Encounter

All teams were sent a notice to return early. Within an hour, the last of the group arrived.

Scout Archer called an assembly. "Scouts, we have new information to share. Samples have been analyzed and visual data confirmed. Apparently, the towers, or something around those rock pillars, that we have always known to be a part of this planet...are alive."

A rumble of shock and disbelief erupted.

"Quiet. Here is the evidence. Samples taken by all teams were uploaded daily to Alpha's Exploratory Branch. Images and seismic data were analyzed chronologically as well as hundreds of material samples. Atmospheric conditions, humidity, spore count—everything was taken into consideration.

"It has been confirmed that the data samples from and around the towers are biological. On top of that, Scouts Estavines and Triton discovered the actual appearance of one new tower which was accompanied by seismic activity. Sample results proved that the injuries to their feet are the result of a type of hydrochloric acid."

Another rumble of voices.

"Bottom line, Scouts, we have possibly discovered another fauna living on Jedira."

Braven recalled his past encounters with the first fauna or monster.

One Scout asked, "Do you mean to say that a creature has lived undetected on this planet longer than humanoids have been here?"

"That's what it looks like. But this creature is not a typical fauna that humanoids are accustomed to knowing. It was believed that the towers were rock, so there has been no analysis done until now."

Looks of question mixed with concern blanketed the group.

"Wait. Do you mean the rock towers are alive?" another Scout asked with disbelief.

After a moment, the answer came. "That's exactly what I'm saying."

Gasps of disbelief. Numerous questions and concerns arose.

"Are they dangerous?"

"We need to leave."

"We're surrounded by them."

"What do we do now?"

Director Archer raised his hands. "We will know much more as time goes on. We now know more about what we are working with, so with our data, we will be departing soon. Everyone is dismissed. Be ready to leave in two hours."

A creature? The towers? The "rock" towers? Braven was confused. When he was young, his Level 6 Class went to visit the towers as a routine exploratory trip. *But they are just granite. How can a rock be alive?*

The group was somber. Everyone commented on their confusion.

The medication had quickly healed Braven's feet, so he was able to walk. He went to break down his sleeper and ready himself for the short trip to Alpha. His mind wandered into his long-forgotten memories of touching and climbing on the rock towers...or rock creatures. He shuddered.

He dumped his gear near the hilo and took out his personal databoard. He searched through the images he had taken years earlier. He ran across an image of the caprodome after it was captured.

Rock doesn't make sense. Braven could not remove these thoughts from his mind. *What about the flora that grows all over and in the center of them? Those thrive with healthy and vibrant colors whereas the rest of the planet has the same cyan-colored plant-life.*

"So, what are you thinking?"

Braven looked up to see his good Scout friend sit down at the table and slide over close.

"Weston, I don't get it. I'm confused about what Scout Archer said about fauna. The only fauna ever discovered was the caprodome, and there was only one of those."

"That we know of. We don't know everything that the researchers are finding on planet. There are many new flora discovered all the time. Why can't there be fauna or insects somewhere that have been kept hidden from humanoids? There is an entire hemisphere on Jedira that has not been thoroughly researched."

"Why is it taking so long? Humanoids have been here my whole life."

"Well, you know about the spires from your planetary studies of Jedira in your younger classes. I've flown over them, and they are impossible to explore with only horizontal landscape to land. Alliance Scouting Teams have been sent in, but they came up with no good data."

"Right, I remember." Braven peered into the landscape. "This side of the planet was hospitable and tolerant to humanoids."

"And the search for habitable planets and moons is a high priority for the Alliance."

"Right. So, with that type of landscape, it is assumed that there was no fauna on that side of the planet. But this hemisphere could work."

"Yep."

Weston was always so practical. Braven knew what he said was true, but he couldn't fit it into his knowledge of the planet. He also knew that "his" knowledge was not the ultimate, so he tried to accept the possibility of there being more.

A small tremblor began and grew quickly. Everyone grabbed onto something to keep things, and themselves, from flying onto the ground. The vibrations shook Braven's body intensely. Perimeter lights fell. Three sleepers collapsed. Scouts fell to the ground. A large swell in the ground just beside the hilo burst open, throwing dirt and rocks all over the surrounding area.

Imager. Imager. Where's my imager?

Braven grabbed the device that had slid to the back of the table. He opened the finder and captured several images of the episode. While he took the images, he fell onto the ground but kept capturing the scenes.

The tremblor continued for many seconds. Suddenly rocks exploded throughout the swell. Granite pelted the vicinity as onlookers ran for their lives or gawked in disbelief. Pebbles and dust sprayed the entire camp.

Silence. Thick dust hung in the air. Coughing and

calls for help could be heard in the sudden stillness. It was difficult for the humanoids to open their eyes or breathe as the dust swirled around them.

As the dust began to settle, onlookers gasped as they saw that a huge monolith had appeared on the west side of the camp where the hilo had rested. The hilo was pushed onto its front on the opposite side of the swell from Braven. Being so near the camp, the protrusion of the monstrosity was shocking as many Scouts were frozen in their gaze while others had run toward the opposite perimeter fence.

"Help!" A silent voice could be heard in the distance.

Everyone quickly gathered themselves, moved away from the monstrosity, and checked on each other for their safety. There were lots of cuts, bruises, coughing, and fears of more incredulous happenings, but no one sustained any serious injuries.

"Help," the voice called again.

Scout Archer yelled, "let's get everyone away from this thing." The Scouts started quickly moving toward the opposite side of the compound.

"Help."

"Where is that coming from?" Weston asked as he searched.

"Where are you? Who is it?" Scout Archer belted out with his commanding voice.

"Mezlin. I think I'm in the air."

They looked toward the top of the monolith. An arm could be seen waving from the top—about fifteen meters high.

"Are you injured?"

After a few seconds, the Scout relayed that she was not hurt but only covered in slime.

"Scouts, get her down ASAP," Scout Archer ordered.

The hilo had clearly been damaged. The ground beneath it had given way, creating a sinkhole. The tail was seen sticking up out of the hole. The aircraft had settled on its front windshield, covered in debris. The landing gear stuck out from the hull.

"Mezlin, we'll get you down. Hold on tight," the camp director called toward the stranded Scout. He turned to the others. "Find a way to get her down now!"

"Stay off the spongy surface," Braven yelled.

"Everything is spongy and slimy. I keep sinking," Scout Mezlin informed them.

Everyone searched for any tool that could be used to scale the monolith's wall. The scaling rope had already been packed in the hilo which had become inaccessible. Three Scouts searched for ways to get inside the hilo. Timlo brought twine, but it was not strong enough for rappelling.

The director continued talking to Mezlin. He suggested she try to climb down the side.

An arm flung over the side followed by a leg. The

motion of the limbs showed that the surface was too slick to gain footing. The foot disappeared and the Scout's head was seen.

"Everything is slimy. I can't stand up; I keep sinking. This odor is sickening."

Someone suggested to Scout Archer, "What if she jumps? There are enough of us to catch her."

The camp director surmised the height of the monolith, their lack of answers, and knew that a jump would be the only valid immediate solution.

"Scout Mezlin, can you jump? We will station everyone to catch you."

Retching could be heard from above.

"I can't get out of this stuff." Silence. The Scouts heard a scream. Schout Mezlin moaned, vomited, and grunted.

All eyes elevated in anticipation.

"Here I come." She waved an arm over the side. She gagged.

All the Scouts gathered closer toward the rock tower with open arms and lifted eyes to see where she would descend. Within three seconds, a body, screaming in fear, fell over the edge.

Everyone rushed to help in the catch. They stopped.

Mezlin's body slammed against the side of the monolith. She hung upside down as something clung to her leg. She screamed and squirmed to get loose. She twisted to grasp her blade. She sliced and jabbed. She slashed and fell without warning.

The sudden drop startled the onlooking Scouts. They crowded in to break the sudden impact. She landed squarely on top of three Scouts with their arms extended. The force of her descending weight brought the group to the ground.

"Scout Able, get the med kit," Scout Archer commanded.

The group relocated to the far end of the camp. All able-bodied Scouts moved the injured as carefully but as quickly as possible. One Scout was directed to keep his eye on the monolith and make sure it didn't do anything.

The number of groans made everyone wonder who was injured more seriously. Scout Mezlin was totally covered in a slimy film that had begun to irritate her skin. Her left foot was broken. The medic began flushing her skin with liquid immediately.

The three Scouts who tempered the landing were also injured. Weston's hand was broken; another's shoulder was dislocated. Scout Mezlin's impact directly on top of Scout Yaltis broke his neck. He did not move. Scout Able pronounced him deceased.

Braven closely watched the rock tower. *How could this happen? This must be a living organism. Rocks don't move like this.* He paused. *Who knows what else could be on this planet?* He stared intently at the physical structure for any movement. There was none. He took images from all sides. His mind swirled as to what this "creature" could be.

Scout Archer directed the team to continue relocating everything away from the monolith. Everyone that was able gathered the camp and moved one hundred meters away. The perimeter lighting was salvaged and reassembled as a new camp. All reclaimed equipment, sleepers, and personal effects were toted to the new camp. Nothing was left but the damaged hilo and anything unretrievable.

Two Scouts placed Scout Yaltis's body at the rear of their new compound and covered it. There were a couple of cadaver packets in the hilo as standard issue, but they were inaccessible. One could possibly be retrieved soon.

The loss of a teammate was grievous. Sorrow struck each Scout as their minds realized the impact. Some were quiet. Some softly cried. Some worked harder to set up the new compound and ignored the facts. Some walked away alone. Braven's heart hurt. He remembered the few times he had worked directly with the eighteen-year veteran Scout from Earth. He knew his grief would be less severe than others since he had only recently met him. He thought that Scout Mezlin might blame herself for his death. He wondered if there was any way he could help her and the others in their grief. He noticed Weston was clearly affected. Braven thought he would wait until later to talk with him. They all needed their time alone to grieve.

It was getting late, and a meal was needed. Braven readied the evening rations. Only two Scouts partook.

He stopped and observed the scene. He wondered why no one had been more concerned about the monolith erupting into the sky right in the middle of their camp. He asked Weston.

"I don't think any of us even considered it. We are all familiar with the monoliths but not as aggressive creatures. If it had tentacles coming out to snatch us, that would be different."

"It will be dusk soon. Will we be safe here tonight?"

Weston said he had not thought of that. He asked Scout Archer about his plans.

"We'll have two shifts posted tonight. Half the team on each shift. The perimeter fence will safeguard anything that may try to enter, but I only hope nothing else comes out of the ground."

Braven thought it may be a good time for his long-awaited question. "Why do we use a perimeter fence when we know of no mobile creatures on the planet?"

A short pause.

"Scout Hastern, schedule the shifts." The camp

director walked away, ignoring the question.

Braven watched the director then slowly moved his eyes to Weston, who was staring at the departing leader. Braven returned his look to the director and then back to his senior Scout friend.

"Weston?"

Slowly, Weston replied, "I don't know." His eyes never left their leader.

***

Capria descended, leaving a dark world. Kadyen was faint as usual and followed the setting sun for the evening. Wilstor was quickly rising. The splash of stars across the heavens was as beautiful as ever. Braven breathed in deeply and lavished the sight, but the smell of the monolith swirled in his nostrils. He could faintly see the standing structure in the perimeter's lighting. He went to find a place to sleep since he had the second shift.

He lay in a salvaged sleeper that would share with a Scout from first shift. He stared at the moonless sky. His mind blurred; his eyes drooped. Peace.

***

Braven suddenly opened his eyes. *What was that noise?* He sat up with his face skyward. He peered through the translucent sleeper cover across the sky with intent, catching the light from every star or perimeter post. He froze with determination to find the culprit. He saw nothing. He slowly lay down and tried to relax.

Did I just hear something? Is my mind playing tricks? Oh, please, let it be in my mind.

He lay back down but couldn't sleep. He had to put his mind at ease and get up to check on things.

He opened the flap and looked around the camp. No movement. He stepped outside and looked around. *Where was the first shift?* He looked around his sleeper. He walked around the perimeter. No one.

He walked to Weston's sleeper, but no one was inside. He checked the others, but all were empty. He stood and looked around frantically.

Where is everyone?

Then, there it was. A yelp. It was close. Again. Closer.

Braven's breathing increased, and he felt his heart rate soar. He searched for a place to hide, but there was nothing close. The hilo.

A yelp.

He started running toward the damaged aircraft. He passed the perimeter fencing without thinking but realized the power was off. He ran faster.

Another yelp.

The hilo was within a few meters when he felt something grab his leg. He fell to the ground. He screamed. He kicked. He fought with everything he had within him.

"Braven." Weston was shaking his leg to wake him.

Braven had backed into the rear of the sleeper. He shook with fear.

"Braven, it's okay. You're okay." The calming words surrounded Braven's senses. Tears ran down his cheeks. His breathing was uncontrollable.

"Weston?"

"Braven, it's okay. I'm here with you. It was just a nightmare."

Braven lowered his face into his hands and didn't move. His consciousness was on high alert. Adrenaline still flushed through his body. He exhaled heavily.

"Are you okay?"

After a short pause, Braven answered with an affirmative.

"Get yourself together. It's your shift."

Braven slowly returned to reality. He inhaled a couple of heavy breaths and exhaled slowly through his nose. He gathered his thoughts of reality and slowly moved to the entrance. He peeked out the shelter's door to see the bustle of changing shifts. Relief flooded him.

The Scouts scattered throughout camp near the perimeters. The quiet humming of the power surging through the fencing was the only sound in the still, dark night. Wilstor had risen and shared its welcomed bright illumination with them. Braven was thankful for that safety.

"What was that all about?" Weston was concerned for his friend.

"Uh...a nightmare."

"Have you had one of those recently?"

"No, not for a while." Braven pondered the last time he even had a bad dream. "I think it's just being back around this mess."

"I understand. It brings back bad memories. Just remember that we are all here for each other, so hang in there." Weston always had comfort in his voice when it was needed.

Braven remained at his post with Weston. He thought of how his friend had been such a dependable companion for so many years. He appreciated his friendship.

The remainder of the night contained no activity. Wilstor had long gone, and Capria's light peered over the horizon. He decided to put out rations since there were not many takers after the tower incident.

Braven sat quietly at the central table and munched on his morning meal. His mind reflected on how recent events mirrored his early childhood survival. He knew food supplies must be rationed, so he inventoried the stock, made his distribution calculations, and developed a ration strategy. He would present his ideas to the director if their departure was delayed.

"Scouts, we are all saddened by the passing of Scout Yaltis. He was a seasoned Scout and a longtime friend of most of us. He will be missed. Scout Mezlin is in critical condition. She will need evacuation as soon as transport arrives. Contact has been made with Alpha, and evac should begin within three hours. Prepare all supplies and equipment for departure. Dismissed."

Braven checked on the food rations and packed them for transport. He assisted with dismantling the perimeter fencing. He pondered the purpose of the security in this device and how he had not received any answer to his curiosity.

Braven grabbed his imager from his pocket. He took imagery of the camp, the tower, the landscape, and the hilo. He made sure he tele-zoomed the hilo since he had no interest in getting too close to that creature. He photographed supplies that were gathered and the Scouts as they hustled to get everything packed for the evac. He captured the occupied cadaver bag. He paused. He put away his imager.

Braven stood alert as three Scouts dug through the wreckage of the hilo. He watched for any signs of movement or change. Hand radios and supplies inside were lifted out. Ration containers were found and lifted through the side opening. The MiniRover was covered with heavy debris, jammed between the crumpled fuselage and a rock. The hilo's radio equipment for contacting the base camp was under the MiniRover.

Soon the hilo arrived, and the camp was evacuated within minutes. Braven took images of the tower as the aircraft lifted before they accelerated.

He leaned back and took a deep breath. He looked at the other Scouts. There was a sense of concern or uncertainty or bewilderment. Braven was unsure. They had all experienced something that possibly no other humanoid had ever encountered. The loss of Scout Yaltis and Mezlin's injuries were such a slap to the usually lively group. *Where does this group go from here?* The Scouting program was the exploratory arm of the military corps, but this had evolved into more than exploration. *Would the Corps be contacted? Would this affect life on Jedira? What about Alpha? And the other colonies?*

Braven let out a hum. Those around him glanced his way.

"Um, sorry."

A groan was heard from the rear of the hilo. Mezlin was waking. She had been restless. She vomited. Scout Able quickly assisted. Her injuries required much more medical attention than what the team could provide. Braven could not imagine having the injuries he had on his feet all over his body like she had on top of her other injuries.

The hilo landed and was unloaded within minutes. The injured were immediately transported to the medical facility. Everything was counted and restocked in preparation for their next mission. Scout Archer had a short debrief. Afterward, the Scouts were released for two days of relaxation.

Braven went to his unit to clean himself and put away his personal effects. It was late afternoon, but he was exhausted and went to rest.

Section 6

Arrival

The next day, he visited his parents at their labs. He explained very little of what his mission was about; they understood he could not discuss everything. He wanted to talk about the monoliths but knew they were classified for now. He visited Khara, Weston and Mesilia, and a few friends he hadn't seen in a while. He stopped by to see how Scout Mezlin was doing, but she was in critical care. He knew he would hear when he got back to the camp.

Two days flew.

Upon arrival at the Scout offices, Braven was notified of a meeting with all participants of the mission. He briefly reviewed his data so he could report if asked.

Director Fortuna informed the team that Scout Mezlin was in serious condition. She had inhaled the acid, and it had penetrated her skin. She would be absent for a while.

The mission was turned over to the military. The

Scouts' responsibility was to assist when needed. Discussion began and ended then moved to other topics. They were given new assignments in pairs around the colony's perimeter. Braven found that this was a common duty when leadership was waiting for new instructions.

Braven was paired with Scout Rimi Zacor. He was a two-year Scout from Proxima B. He had not gone on the mission, but the two had interacted earlier. Rimi was two years older than Braven with olive skin and brown hair.

Braven and Rimi were sent to the southern region of the colony for a routine appearance. Alphans highly respected the Scouts and were pleased to see them. They talked with many of the locals and enjoyed the company. He felt honored by them. He was impressed with Rimi's attractive personality and how he interacted so well with every colonist. Everyone seemed to like him.

Their day was uneventful. No emergencies, no one to help. They just rode or walked around talking to colonists. Braven concerned himself with watching for ground swells. The entire experience on the mission rattled him somewhat as with the other Scouts. He thought of Scout Yaltis. He wondered how Scout Mezlin had progressed since their return.

That evening, he visited Weston and Mesilia. He was excited about their little arrival. Upon reaching their unit, their windows were open, and he overheard the couple searching for the best name for their child.

"Aquili?"

"No, that sounds like a humanoid from my planet. I do not want to be reminded of him every time I say our child's name."

"Blantar?"

"Really?"

"You two are so amusing." Braven couldn't help but chuckle.

The couple looked up with big smiles and welcomed him into their unit. Soon, Braven was interjecting names, mostly humorous ones.

Mesilia would deliver their baby in thirteen days, which was the end of the Blauken pregnancy. She was excited and knew her baby would be beautiful.

Weston would not discuss Scout business around Mesilia, so Braven didn't mention anything. He thought that was a wise practice. His parents didn't discuss their work too much unless it involved their lives, such as the storms or the planet's flora.

Braven left and went to see his parents. As usual, they were as delighted to see him as if he had gone on a long journey.

"I was just here last night."

"Well, we love seeing you any time." Mom gave him a big hug.

"More bees make the honey sweet," Dad smiled.

Braven couldn't help but laugh. "Where did you hear that phrase?"

Dad laughed. "I was researching something at work and that appeared. It means the more family around, the better it is. It was an archaic phrase from Eden's past." Dad had recently started looking into odd metaphors and old trivia. Braven thought it was his way of being humorous.

After their time together, Braven walked back to his unit. The evening was nice, but he couldn't see as many stars as usual. He realized that he was near a solar lamp. He walked a little farther, but there was another. He didn't remember seeing so much light in the colony at night. He examined the lamps and saw that they had recently been placed. As he walked farther toward his unit, he realized new lamps were placed every four meters. This illuminated every section of the area. Braven thought it was nice, but he enjoyed the quiet ambience of the fading light.

***

The next day at their morning meeting, Director Fortuna announced that Scout Mezlin had passed early in the morning due to her injuries. Shock was evident in everyone's expression. He then introduced Dr. Gostrinsa and explained she was a grief counselor who would like to speak with each Scout.

Braven appreciated her availability. He remembered

his earlier counseling and how relevant and comforting it was to him during his last encounter. He decided he would allow the others who were closer to Yaltis and Mezlin meet with her first.

Assignments were continued for another day. Director Fortuna allowed time with the counselor as needed.

Braven and Rimi traveled to the southern neighborhoods. They found perimeter fencing had been recently erected in that area by the Construction Corps. They also discovered that the Corps planned to surround the colony with the protective barrier.

Why would they put up a fence when the creature came up from the ground? Why a fence? Are the new lamps in case of possible caprodomes? Why didn't Scout Archer answer his question about the perimeter? Do they expect the creature to come this far north?

Another day of visiting with colonists and enjoying the day in the southern region. The colony had roughly five thousand inhabitants. Braven knew none of them from this area and was able to make new friends.

That evening was typical. Braven stayed around his unit which was near the other Scouts. At times, he could hear someone walk by and call to him. They would talk about nothing and return to their solitude.

Three days passed and their assignments remained

the same. Braven and Rimi visited the different zones of their assigned area. Each had interesting inhabitants. Many welcomed them as they arrived in their rover. The children asked if they could have a ride. Rimi loved the children and happily relented. They screamed with joy as he turned in circles.

Braven saw Rimi as a fun and bright humanoid. He enjoyed his company and was always impressed with his positive attitude. He had fun in most situations.

After the joyride, Rimi secured the rover, and they walked through the area. The new lamps and fencing had been erected earlier. They checked to make sure the caution fence was three meters from the perimeter so children would not get too close. All was sound.

Another day of normal duty. They were ready to return to the rover when it happened.

Braven stopped.

The ground beneath him trembled and then stopped.

"What was that?" one citizen questioned.

"Was that another groundquake?" another local asked as he looked around with caution.

Looks of concern were on all faces. Groundquakes were rare on Jedira, at least where the colonies were located.

Braven asked what they meant by "another"

groundquake.

"Did you not feel that one last night? It was light but I felt it."

"I felt it, too."

"So did I."

He surveyed the area for any ground swell. Nothing.

The Scouts surveyed the area. They looked for any sign of danger so they could warn the Alphans. Braven walked around buildings and into the street. There were no changes to the ground.

Braven retrieved his N-Line and notified base camp of the event. They had heard from two other Scouts in the western region with the same report. He was ordered to stay in the vicinity, and someone would arrive shortly with sensors.

Two colonists questioned the groundquakes. He said he reported it, and someone was coming to place sensors. That made them feel comfortable. He was glad they didn't know the reason for those quakes.

Within ten minutes, two Scouts arrived via hilo. Braven and Rimi helped them place sensors in strategic locations. Braven used the imager they had and captured numerous digiphotos of the surrounding area. He made sure the images overlapped.

They stayed in the area for another two hours to ensure everything was okay, then they returned in the rover to camp.

Upon arrival, there was an urgent meeting for all available Scouts. Director Fortuna discussed the situation and asked for responses. Braven realized that all the Scouts knew of the mission details.

Scout Archer asked, "why is seismic activity this close to Alpha? Does that mean one of those monoliths are coming here?"

"Don't jump to conclusions, we are here to keep all colonists safe." Director Fortuna spoke calmly to the group. "We are placing sensors and cameras all around the colony. We should know long before they ever get here."

"Does that mean they are coming here?" another Scout asked.

"I didn't say that. We need to be ready to protect the colonists if that happened."

"Director." One of the Scouts from the Comm Center entered and directed him to his databoard. The director took one look and announced that another tremblor had happened in the southwest region.

"We need Scouts on the ground for surveillance. Scout Acher, assign continuous teams, especially in the southern and western regions. Dismissed."

Braven was again paired with Rimi. They had the night shift in the southwest region beginning at 2100. They packed their gear and took off in the rover toward their destination.

Why couldn't I have gotten the day shift? I pray that Wilstor will be shining brightly tonight. Braven remembered the dark nights and the terror that came with them.

The lamps brightened up the area well. Very few colonists were walking about. Many sat on their front stoops, some were visiting with neighbors. Laughter erupted at times from one unit. The atmosphere was welcoming and relaxing. It felt like home.

The pair drove around the perimeter. Nothing was unusual. They found an area where they could view most of the region—a building located close to the perimeter that had an upper deck. They climbed up and stood at the edge. A light had been erected on top of that building's corner near the exterior fencing.

The night was peaceful. The quiet hum of the fencing was the only constant noise. They sat in the corner on top of the building, legs dangling, facing the colony. Braven faced one direction while Rimi the other. Solar lamps glowed over the entire area.

They sat quietly for hours only making random comments. Their databoards and N-Lines were quiet. The wind was fractional. The usual faint smells of flora and water from the night mists surrounded their nostrils.

"I could take a nap about now," Rimi yawned.

Braven looked at his companion.

"Well, we already worked all day. But, of course, I won't. We're on duty."

Braven felt relieved that Rimi was not just all fun but had a responsible side as well. He chuckled.

Hours passed with no change. The two surveyed the same scenery.

"Let's walk around, or I will take a nap," Rimi stated as he stood and stretched.

Braven thought it was a good idea to stretch his legs anyway. They walked through the streets being careful not to approach any unit and disturb the resting inhabitants. There were no disturbances until they received a notification from camp of their relief.

The pair was thankful for their shift to end. They had not rested for a full day. Both returned to camp, found their units, and ended their long double shift.

The next evening was the same. They returned to the southwest region for another long and boring night shift. Capria touched the horizon. The rise was beautiful from the top of the building, where they made their personal headquarters.

As they waited for their shift relief, they heard a colony-wide alarm sound. Braven looked up and surveyed the area. Their N-Lines alerted them with an urgent message. He opened the message to see that a monolith had risen in Alpha's southern region. They got in their rover and headed toward the incident.

Upon arriving, the pair saw an enormous monolith of forty meters standing in the location of a former family unit. The colonists gawked at the site, unable to fully take in the event. They had never seen a gigantic monolith appear from the ground. The emanating odor reeked horribly. Fear struck, as no one knew what had happened.

Braven and Rimi joined Weston and another Scout with a dozen onlookers. A crowd gathered around the Scouts to find out answers. Weston took charge. He asked if anyone was injured. Unfortunately, the inhabitants of the unit could not be found.

Weston got their attention. "We are not sure what is going on. We will find out. In the meantime, stay clear of this thing. If your unit is in the vicinity, do not return until farther instructions. Shelter will be provided further away. Do not go near that thing."

Weston updated base camp. He requested a shelter be established for several families. Within minutes, he was informed that a sanctuary had been secured at one of the administrative buildings near the Southern Commons. Military units were notified to assist.

Within two hours, all families living near the monolith had been relocated to the shelter and provided with what they needed. The surrounding area was cordoned off within one hundred meters of the monstrosity. Director Fortuna had a perimeter established, and fencing was erected around the monolith. Two guards were assigned to remain on patrol at the monolith and to immediately report any changes in the situation.

Military teams from the Alliance landed. They assumed command in an organized fashion. Braven was impressed with their efficiency and how they seemed to know each other's thoughts. The Scouts were relieved of their patrols and were directed to assist any straggling colonists to be relocated. They returned to their camp to await further instructions. They were all placed on high alert with half-day shifts.

Braven was glad the military arrived. They were the protectors of the planets. Two of his childhood friends departed for military training as Braven left for the Academy. The Corps was focused, very professional, and highly regarded by all.

***

The Central Commons was crowded as humanoids from all over the colony gathered. Concerns of invasion and destruction flooded voices.

"What are you going to do?" a gray-haired female asked with a stern glare. "Do we just wait around until one of those things takes our unit and family into the air like what happened to that family?"

"We do not believe more of this type of thing will happen." The colony director was absolute. "These monoliths have never presented a danger to any humanoid."

"How can we be assured of that?" another colonists asked

"We want our families safe," yelled a female from the rear of the crowd.

"Please." Director Motsla raised his hands. "Don't rush into fear. Our scientists, Scouts, theorists, and military are all involved in finding an answer. We must be patient and let decisions be made."

"What can we do in the meantime?" asked a Radzierian male.

A slight pause. "Carry on with your duties. Be cautious, and report anything unusual to your local authorities. The N-Line is continually active so stay in tune. Skysight drones have been monitoring the entire colony since the event and will continue as long as needed. Military personnel have been dispatched to regions outside and surrounding the perimeter. Everyone is working to find answers."

General Artula approached the director.

"Please hear from General Artula." The director was noticeably relieved to have the military commander take over.

The crowd silenced as the commander approached the speaker's podium. Her demeanor and presence seemed to demand respect from the crowd.

"We are confident that the situation is under control. Troops have been assigned continually and will be located throughout the colony. As Director Motsla stated, Skysight continually covers the entire colony and within one hundred meters outside the perimeter. Within the colony, Scouts are available for assistance to Director Motsla. Please report all unusual activities of any kind to the authorities in your region. The worst that can happen is for any of us to fall into fear of the unknown," she continued.

Braven viewed the crowd and saw his parents. They nodded in agreement at the general's statements. He was concerned about their being in danger.

After the crowd was dismissed, Braven made his way through the crowd to see his parents. They were happy for a family reunion even though they had seen each other two days earlier. Comments and concerns were exchanged.

"Please be alert around you. This is the second monolith we have seen sprout up like that, but nothing seems to happen afterward. Hopefully, it is just the way these things grow." Braven thought his comfort to them was an odd change from their comfort to him throughout his life.

"We all thought they were rock, but now we don't

know what they are? What initiates them to spring up, and where is their central processor located." Dad was searching for answers.

Braven wished he had more information, but he was a lower-classified Scout and only privy to certain data. *I wonder if Weston knows anything more about this.*

***

Two days passed. The military and Scouts conducted continuous monitoring of the monolith. There were no changes. The emanating smell grew stronger at times but not to a putrid state.

The colonist's emotions about the tower calmed. It became ignored while other topics invaded conversations. Some ventured close to the established perimeter, while others questioned why they couldn't move back into their units.

Even Braven thought that it may be how the towers were formed, and it was unfortunate for their camp and this house to be in that location when it erupted from the ground. No harm had come to the colony except that unit.

On the third day after the eruption, Director Motsla gave the order to release the perimeter so colonists could return to their units for personal effects.

Section 7

Infiltration

Braven opened his N-Line to see a personal message from his mother.

Mom: Braven, did you say that there were dozens of monoliths on your mission?

Me: Yes.

Mom: Were they of various sizes?

Me: Yes.

Mom: Was that odor stronger in that area?

Me: Yes.

Mom: And the one that erupted on your mission, was it near any others?

Me: Yes.

Mom: Do you say anything but "yes"?

Me: HAHA. Yes.

There was a long pause.

Me: Mom, is everything okay?

Mom: Yes.

Me: Do you think these things are connected somehow?

Mom: Yes.

Me: Do you say anything but "yes"?

Mom: HAHA. I think I have a theory. Thanks.

End Communication.

Braven went to visit his mother at her research lab. Their short N-Line communication made him curious, and he planned on finding out what she knew. When he arrived, she was examining specimens.

"Hi, Mom."

"Hey, Braven."

"What is your theory? Maybe I can help."

"I need to do some more investigating. Things are not working in the typical manner." Mom looked back into her microscope.

"What do you mean?"

"I must think about this situation outside of my main mode of investigation."

"Mom?"

"I just can't put my finger on it."

"Mom!"

The scientist raised her head. Her eyes looked

beyond her son.

"Mom?"

"Oh, I'm here." She came to herself. "This isn't normal. Let's talk about this. Can you come over tonight before you go to your shift? I believe you, Dad, and I need to put our heads together."

"In the meantime, it was good to see you." Braven displayed an innocent smirk.

"You give me a hug and go get some rest." Mom's hugs were always so warm and sincere.

***

That evening, about three hours before his shift, Braven arrived at his parents' unit. They sat and discussed all the events that had happened recently as well as in years past. Each of them explained in detail anything that may relate to the monoliths and their possible migration toward the colony.

Braven evaluated, "at Delta Colony, there were a few monoliths scattered around the region. While at Zeta Colony, there were more of them. Here at Alpha, there are very few. In the southern region, they are numerous."

Braven took out his databoard. He drew a simple sketch of the location of the colonies. Alpha was the central colony. Delta was five hundred kilometers east of Alpha. Zeta was twelve hundred kilometers to the southeast and across the Grand Chasm. The Grand Chasm stretched for more than two thousand kilometers, about six hundred kilometers away from the colony from the west of Alpha to the southeast.

Dad piped in. "The towers are more prevalent in the southern region below the Chasm."

Braven added in places where monoliths were congregated. "Why are there so many monoliths in some places and very few in others?"

"If they reproduce, they must be autogenic."

"Wait." Braven was stumped by his mom's statement. "How are these things classified? Flora or fauna?"

"We need to determine whether the monoliths are fauna or flora." Mom held up one finger. "We know they are not gabbro or granite as we earlier suspected."

"Do they reproduce?" Dad had a curious facial expression.

Braven looked at his father. He had never thought of the monoliths as anything but rocks.

Mom continued, "we are on a planet we do not know everything about. Remember how on Radzier—the planet not the star—flora is red rather than cyan as it is here, and it is green on Eden and Earth. That's because the chlorophyll has a different structure on Radzier and Jedira. Therefore, we must think that the normal process may be inaccurate for this planet."

Braven pondered her point. He wondered how bizarre this could become.

"So, let's say that all these monoliths are related to a central figure. Maybe the 'Great Mother' is located in the south where most of the monoliths are." Dad emphasized the name he created.

Braven looked back at the databoard. "But how do they travel? How do they know where to go? And why would they move in one specific direction?"

Mom stared at the two males with a blank countenance. She slowly raised her finger.

"I have found some unknown matter in the ground's substrate. I also saw it at Delta and Zeta. I conferred with others, but we have never understood what that could be except part of the planet's soil compound. I have obtained many samples and run numerous tests, but I always draw a blank when compared to what we know about other planets."

"Do you think this substrate has anything to do with the monolith growth?"

Mom's brain was working overtime. She quietly mumbled as the other two stared at her. She stood up and walked in circles.

"Dad, is she okay?"

"She started this a few years back when she is in deep thought. I just ignore her because she won't hear me."

"Oh!" Mom burst out.

The males responded in unison.

Mom looked like she had a revelation.

"Mycelium!"

"What's that?"

"Mycelium is how a flora can interact over a large distance. Fungus on Eden can spread their mycelia for thousands of kilometers and cover the entire planet. Earth has some, but it is more centralized. They are near-microscopic root fibers and are scattered all over those two planets. At any time, a sprig from any location can sprout. Sometimes it depends on the need of the source. Another sprig may grow hundreds of kilometers away from the same 'Great Mother' source."

All were impressed with the information. They came up with dozens of phenomena and conclusions.

"I need to do some more testing and inform Director Motsla and the general."

Braven looked at his databoard; it was time for his shift.

***

Hours lapsed as Rimi and Braven Scouted the southern region for any activity. It had been almost five days since the monolith arrived and nothing of any urgency had evolved. The perimeter was still established. They got out of their rover and walked around the area. As usual, the night was peaceful. They met with two military guards who were surveying the region west of the monolith. They chatted for a while, and then the Scouts left and walked back toward the stone pillar.

Braven caught a quiet sound. He stopped walking and turned his head toward the perimeter. "Did you hear something?"

Rimi looked around but said he heard nothing out of the ordinary.

Braven made his way toward the sound which was in the direction of the monolith. He approached the perimeter and listened intently.

There it was again. A very soft squeak.

"Did you catch that?"

Rimi frowned. "I did."

They scoured the monolith on all sides and listened closely.

Nothing.

After a few minutes, Rimi asked, "Do you think we were just imagining it?"

"I don't think we could imagine the same thing at the same time."

Rimi took out his databoard and reported the incident to the base. The two remained at the monolith until Capria and their replacements arrived. The two returned to base and retired from their nightly duties.

That afternoon, Braven was awakened by an N-Line alert which informed him that two more monoliths sprung up just to the west of the earlier one. Director Fortuna scheduled a meeting in one hour.

"More?"

At the meeting, the director detailed current events. Groundquakes increased in the south and west of the colony. Three more monoliths had appeared. One appeared inside the colony next to the first and took down a large section of perimeter fencing toppling a building. No one was injured this time. The other two appeared just outside the perimeter to the west.

"The problem is that we don't know what these things are nor why they are approaching Alpha the way they are. Director Motsla is contemplating a colony evacuation."

At that, gasps filled the room. Questions from the group began.

"Evacuate five thousand humanoids?"

"In what timeframe is he thinking?"

"He is only considering it. Of course, he will have advice from his officials. Department heads are all aware, and everyone is working together to determine the best course of action. In the meantime, we need to prepare ourselves to help the colonists."

He continued his discussion and ended with wanting

to see Braven and Rimi.

The two Scouts met the director at his lectern. Weston was present; Braven had not seen his friend much since he was placed on night shift. The director wanted more information about the sound they heard.

Rimi told him his rendition but said Braven heard it first.

"Scout Triton, did that sound remind you of anything?"

Braven thought. "No, sir. It was just a tiny squeak. I thought it was material hanging from one of the damaged buildings."

"Scout Zacor, you are released. Scout Triton, please join me." The director walked toward the left door. Rimi and Braven glanced at each other, and Braven followed his senior. Weston trailed them.

They entered the communications room where Braven had never been. The walls were filled with screens displaying dozens of scenes of the colony and outside the perimeter. A communications Scout directed him to watch a specific screen. He explained to Braven that the visual was of the top of the first monolith inside the perimeter. She started the video, and Braven focused.

The top of the monolith was solid like the others he had seen. He knew they were spongy and slimy.

"What am I looking for?"

"Just watch."

The surface was as stationary as any other surface looked. Then he noticed something moved.

"What was that?"

"Exactly what I want to know."

Braven drew closer to the monitor. The movement stopped, then started again.

"Can you replay that and zoom in?"

The Scout drew in the picture. She paused and increased the terapixels.

Braven focused on where the movement originated. His eyes widened. He froze. He couldn't breathe. Braven leaned back still with widened eyes and opened mouth.

"Scout Triton?"

He tried to speak but nothing came out. He turned toward the director and gasped.

"That's a caprodome!"

Section 8

Invasion

Braven hyperventilated.

"Scout Triton, calm down. You're okay." The director tried to ease the discovery.

"Sir, we are not okay. That thing will destroy us all." Braven spoke out of breath.

"Scout Triton." The director spoke with an elevated voice. "Get ahold of yourself." The stern expression on his face emphasized his words.

"Braven, you are safe." Weston used his calming voice. "It's important that we know all we can about this thing."

Braven breathed deeply, raised his head toward the ceiling, and closed his eyes.

"Yes, sir. I'm fine. I was not expecting to see that."

"As Scout Hastern stated, we need to know everything you know. We know it's a caprodome, but why and how did it get there?"

Braven looked at the screen, then toward the floor. His breathing calmed. "I need to sit down."

The three Scouts left the Comm room and entered a small conference room. The center table allowed for ten individuals. As they entered, the director input into his databoard. They all sat at the end of the table where they could easily talk. Within the minute, in walked two other individuals. Braven recognized one as his former counselor, but he did not recognize the other.

"Scout Triton, I believe you know Dr. Sinclair." Director Fortuna motioned toward the doctor.

The counselor smiled with the deep warmth that Braven had grown to know.

"This is Dr. Valtera; he is the Director of Interplanetary Zoology. He arrived yesterday from Eden." He turned to the doctor and continued. "Thank you, Dr. Valtera, for joining us so quickly."

The distinguished gentleman nodded. His demeanor was serious.

"Scout Triton, we have read your bio and know the events from Zeta Colony. I need you to tell us everything you know about this creature."

Why is everyone reading my bio? Braven was still shaken from the initial shock. He searched his memory, then realized that the Alliance had captured the original monster. Why didn't they study it themselves?

"Don't you still have the one from years ago? The Alliance captured it and sent it somewhere off planet. Did you study it?"

The counselor seemed uneasy.

Dr. Valtera stated, "We studied the creature but need to know your experience with it. Can you tell us about your initial encounter?"

Braven thought for a moment, exhaled, then began.

"It was years ago at Zeta Colony. Weston and I were at the mining camp and saw it coming out of a cave. It only appeared during the dark, so we didn't get a good look at it. When the miners put me in the cave, I heard it deeper inside. After I got out and hid, it came out and flew away. The next morning, it came back to the cave. I was hiding in the flora, and it didn't see me."

Braven looked at the doctors as he summarized all he knew.

"How did it sound? Smell?" Dr. Valtera seemed deeply interested.

Without hesitation, Braven responded, "It stunk, worse than anything I had smelled. Really sickening. Like what we smelled on our recent mission.

"Can you describe it, and does it make noise?" Dr. Valtera was inputting data while asking.

Braven thought. "It looked like a large Radzierian asp but sounded like turps."

"Turps?" Director Fortuna questioned.

"A small fauna on Eden. I used to play with them when I lived there."

"I see. Did you ever touch the creature?" Dr. Valtera redirected the topic.

"The caprodomes? Never."

The interview continued with questions Braven had never considered. The doctor brought up the time he had touched a monolith on the side of the mountain during a school exploration trip at Zeta. Braven had forgotten that incident. *How did he know about that?* He asked where he thought the creature lived or originated. Braven did not know that answer.

The doctor continued and occasionally asked Weston for details about his comments. After a little longer, Braven and Weston were released, leaving the others in the room.

"What was that all about?"

"Just an inquiry. They interviewed me before the Scout meeting and asked if I would join you to help clarify events."

"I can't believe there are three more monoliths," Braven turned as they talked. "That makes five in the last month that we know of. What is going on?"

"Everyone is trying to figure that out."

Braven prepared himself for his shift. He and Rimi

were sent toward the western region. They visited with military patrol, but their shift was uneventful.

After his shift, Braven visited his mother at her lab. He asked her if she had discovered any new evidence. He told her about the three new monoliths and his interview. She said she was still analyzing the soil samples she had from the three locations with the sample she received from the Scout mission.

"You have that data?"

"Of course. My department researches all data involving flora, detritus, and soil compounds." Mom smirked. "That is what we do here."

That made sense to Braven. He had not thought about her involvement with the colony officials.

"The department heads had a meeting this morning about the new formations. I think I may have some connection but still have questions."

"Can you tell me?"

"Do you remember the mycelia on Eden that I discussed? Jedira has the same thing. Samples from all over the accessible part of the planet have the same types of compounds. It looks like the areas where samples have been taken have the same network. Mycelia thrives abundantly on this planet. It's just that it isn't in the same structure as typical mycelia."

"Why is that important?" Braven questioned.

"That means that the monolith structures are living organisms. And not many organisms but only one. Dad was correct in calling it the 'Great Mother' because that's basically what it is."

"What? How is that possible? They are separated by thousands of kilometers."

"Well, there is a type of central nervous system in this flora..."

"Flora? It's a plant?" Braven was baffled.

"Yes, I believe the monoliths are a type of flora on this planet, a type that we have never encountered. Most flora are independent and produce offspring through seeds but can also spread through asexual vegetative reproduction. In other words, they can be produced by using root tubers or rhizomes. However, I believe the monoliths can reproduce via a type of stolon. These are long internodes that allow more shoots to form. Come look at this."

Mom looked in her microscope and adjusted the knob. She backed away for her son. He peered in to see a cellular structure.

"What am I looking at?"

Mom explained the cell and its internal structures.

"That cell has a typical flora makeup, but it contains cilia which are only found in fauna cells. Cilia are used for locomotion."

"So, these are a mix of flora and fauna cells?"

"Exactly. That cell type is rare at most on any planet. I'm still researching the outcome behind this finding." She looked back into her microscope.

Braven was interested but wanted to tell her about his interview.

"Mom, I saw a digiphoto of a caprodome."

"Really?" She seemed absorbed in her discovery.

"Mom. I saw a digiphoto of a real caprodome. It wasn't from years ago."

Mom stopped and looked at her son.

"What are you talking about?"

"Just now, I was at the Comm Center, and they showed me. It's in the top of the monolith."

"The top of the monolith? But that would be in the light, and caprodomes do not like the light."

"Exactly, but how and why would it be there?"

Mom thought for a moment. "What are they going to do?"

"They didn't say."

"On that topic, I was thinking about that monster. We wondered why there was only one. Why not a mate? I believe I have a theory. I was going to present it to the director but wanted more evidence. Some florae can produce monokaryotic mycelia, and some fauna asexually reproduce. I wonder if the caprodomes are the same."

"You think it was a female, and there are no male caprodomes!"

"In a sense. If caprodomes are considered females, they could asexually lay fertilized eggs."

"But where do the caprodomes come from in the first place?" Braven had a stern expression. "That caprodome was on the top of the tower."

Mom thought. "Not sure. When was that digiphoto taken?"

"Evidently after we reported hearing a sound early this morning."

"You heard it? This morning?"

"Yes, Mom. You and Dad need to stay out of the dark. Remember, the caprodomes don't like the light."

Braven left for his shift. The night shift was as unmemorable as ever—quiet and with only an occasional guard or military to drop by. Rimi and Braven discussed where they would be if they had no other responsibilities. They dreamed of enchanted planets in faraway galaxies. Braven mentioned his two Academy buddies who were assigned together for the excitement of a lifetime while he was stuck on this planet. Rimi wanted to meet his perfect mate and settle on Eden. Soon their replacements arrived.

Braven wanted to get some rest and see what his parents had discovered before he reported for his night shift. As he headed to his unit, he thought he felt the ground move. Was *that a groundquake? Those have only been in the southern region.* He took his databoard to report. He detoured by the Scout camp to see if it was an actual incident.

"A monolith rose one hundred meters from the Central Commons," Scout Archer mentioned as Braven arrived.

The Central Commons was the center of the entire colony. The monoliths had invaded the colony's interior. All Scouts were dispatched to the Commons to assist the colonists.

When he and other Scouts arrived, they could not believe the sight. Two monoliths had burst through the ground. One was the normal elevated height, but the other was only two meters tall. The Colonists were in shock to see these towers.

The military had already established a perimeter. The Scouts helped to keep the colonists away from the area. The smaller monolith raised the edge of one unit but caused little damage. The larger one had risen in an open area.

"Weston, what is going on?"

"You know as much as I do. It looks like at any time one of these things could rise anywhere. I hope no one is standing in the way."

After everything had calmed, most of the Scouts

returned to camp. There was an impromptu meeting about a possible planetary evacuation. More details would be shared as they were received. The shifts were to continue until further notice, so Braven was released for some rest.

He lay with his eyes closed. His mind swirled. *A caprodome is here in Alpha? And, of course, I have night shift.* He exhaled. What would he do if he encountered one at night? He knew he needed some rest before his shift began. He looked at his databoard. Six hours. He sat up. He thought he would go visit his parents and see if they found out anything.

***

"But how did an infant caprodome get on the top of the monolith?" Braven asked his mother.

"Maybe the mother dropped the egg or the baby itself there?" Mom shrugged.

"Why would it do that?" Dad mumbled.

Braven shook his head. "There are no reports of caprodomes until this digiphoto, so where is the mother? And when did she deposit the baby? And how did it get on top of the monolith?"

Dad interrupted. "What if the towers carry caprodome egg to wherever they sprout? The monolith needs the food, and the caprodomes are successful in finding it."

Mom pointed her finger at Dad. "You have a good

point. Like a symbiosis."

Dad winked and grinned at Braven.

"You still have it, Dad."

"You just say it because it's true!"

Mom ignored the comments. "What if there was a symbiotic relationship between the monolith and the caprodomes? The towers could be the digestive appendages for the parent creature. The caprodomes would put food items in the top for the creature to digest." She thought a moment, then muttered, "But what does the caprodome get from this?" She began walking in circles.

Braven looked at his dad. Dad shrugged and grinned.

While she was pondering, Braven told his dad that there were rumors of evacuation from the colony and maybe the planet.

"That would be a huge endeavor. There are about five thousand humanoids in Alpha and another fifteen hundred or so at the other three colonies."

"Do you think they would do that?"

"Possibly. It depends on how critical the situation is, but it can be done."

"That would take a long time with nearly seven thousand humanoids."

"Well, how do you eat an elephant?" Dad smirked.

Braven turned to his father and felt stumped on how

to respond. He finally got his voice to speak. "What's an elephant?"

"Oh, it was a gigantic fauna on ancient Earth. Largest land animal at the time. I read about it recently."

"Humanoids ate elephants?"

"It's just an analogy."

"What does eating an elephant have to do with this evacuation?" Braven was puzzled.

"Forget the elephant. Let's get started."

"Did ancient Terrans not have enough food, so they ate elephants?"

Dad looked at his son. "To finish a big project, you take small steps until the job is complete. Take one bite at a time of the huge elephant, or the big project, and soon it will be eaten, or completed."

"Did Terrans eat other fauna? What about other humanoids?"

"Braven."

A smile came across the Scout's face. "Were Terrans cannibals?" Braven laughed.

Dad closed his eyes and shook his head.

Mom suddenly interrupted. "What if caprodomes were offspring of the monolith creature? Maybe the offspring are obligated to feed the parents like the dray moths on Eden. I need to talk to a zoologist, or maybe biologist. This is a hypothesis worth researching."

Dad winked at Braven. "I knew she would figure something out."

"Do you think we could eat the caprodomes?"

Braven and Dad laughed aloud.

Section 9

Encroachment

Braven saw the notification of a meeting concerning an immediate partial evacuation. He quickly made his way to the meeting.

All non-essential personnel were to be evacuated to the Jediran space portal within the next seventy hours. Braven had never seen so many humanoids scurrying around the colony. The evacuees were only allowed to take one bag carrying their clothing and personal items.

Braven contacted his parents via N-View. Both were considered essential only because they were their department's directors. Mesilia was considered essential since her position was medical, but because her baby was arriving within the next two days, she would be placed on first evac as soon as the baby arrived. Weston stayed near Mesilia as the physician prepared for the delivery.

The Scouts assisted the military in the evacuation. The air shuttle arrived and returned to the space portal at regular intervals. Another air shuttle was dispatched to join in the evacuation. Every two to three hours, one of the shuttles was loaded and departed with just over two hundred humanoids to the safety of the space portal. The evacuation seemed like a well-organized event.

Another groundquake. Everyone looked around to see if the ground would burst open to reveal a new monolith. The eruption happened near the research labs. N-Line messages were full of distress and sightings of new towers that made their way above the surface.

Braven was concerned for his parents. He had not seen or heard from them in many hours. There were no replies to his messages.

An air shuttle was loading for departure, so he requested permission to check on his parents. Since there was adequate personnel available, he was allowed to leave.

He arrived at the research buildings and froze. A tower had erupted under the center of the structure and divided the building. Braven ran to find his parents.

Humanoids were scurrying in and around the building's remains to search for coworkers. Braven's heart dropped. He feared the worst. He N-Lined the Comm Center.

He ran to the entrance closest to his mother's lab. The doors were broken off their hinges, but the opening was clear. He edged inside and called for his parents. He could hear noises from others clearing debris as he made his way toward her lab.

That section of the building seemed quite ragged. The interior doors were partly open. He struggled and gradually opened them enough to reveal a chaotic mess. Displays were smashed on the floor, tables were overturned, and parts of the ceiling had fallen.

"Mom!"

No response.

"Mom!" Braven sounded louder.

His anxiety grew quickly.

He searched under tables and furniture. He scanned the room for any possibility of her being there. Nothing.

Maybe she got out. Dad!

He left that lab and turned to the left toward his father's lab. The hallway was impassable. Braven's mind swirled.

Where can they be? Please be okay! Please be okay!

He tried the other side of the building. He ran out the door, around the building, and circled the newly surfaced monolith. Dad's lab was farther from the center of the building and looked less damaged. He ran.

Inside the building, Braven entered his father's lab. He found his dad assisting two injured coworkers who were hurt when the structure's ceiling caved in.

"Dad!"

"Braven. Help me get these two outside the building. We need to move, and she can't walk."

Braven quickly assessed the situation and picked up the injured female. He carried her while his father assisted the other female to escape the building. They made their way from the building and toward the Central Commons. A soldier saw them and called for another to assist them. The two military personnel took the victims toward safety.

"Dad, I can't find Mom."

"Have you checked her lab?"

"Yes."

"She may have gotten out with the first group of rescuers. Let's go find out."

The two searched and questioned others. Braven sent a message about their plight to the Scout's communication center. They circled the building and tower and found one male unconscious. They contacted help and continued their search after assistance arrived. They peered into windows of rooms they could not access. They returned to her lab but had no success.

They left the building, found the nearest military personnel, and explained their situation. She alerted the Command Center. No results.

"Where could she be?" Braven was worried. He could see the look of dismay on his father's face.

"Dad, we are going to find her."

After a little hesitation, his father responded positively but with uncertainty.

They searched for a little longer. Dad suggested she may have gone to their unit. They made shortcuts behind buildings to arrive quickly.

Upon first sight, they froze in their tracks. A five-meter monolith stood at the side of the structure. Their unit had been toppled.

Despair blanketed them. They ran to the scene and peered through a window to see their personal possessions dumped and scattered. They ran around the roof to the other side. Braven climbed to look inside.

"There's Mom!"

He quickly cleared the opening so he could crawl inside. Carefully stepping on top of broken furniture, he made his way to get to his mother. His heart sank. Mom was pinned under part of the interior wall. He quickly felt her pulse.

"Dad, I need help."

Dad had just finished an emergency N-Line about their situation. He tried getting through the window but was not as agile as his son.

"How is she? Help will be here in a minute."

"She's pinned under the structure. Her pulse is good, but she is unconscious."

Dad placed a follow-up message. Within three

minutes, two guards arrived. One quickly jumped into the window to assist. The other began making his way inside. Another minute later, a team of three military arrived. The group gathered around the fallen wall and hoisted it while Braven and a guard pulled the female to safety.

Mom was carefully carried outside the unit. She was whisked away by a medical transport before Braven could crawl out of the unit.

Braven and Dad scurried to the medical facility. As they arrived, the medics were taking Mom to triage. The two waited and watched.

Another groundquake. Windows popped. Screams erupted. The wall behind them heaved. Dad landed on top of Braven who had already been knocked to the floor. The structure had been slightly tilted but was still stable.

The two recovered and went to check on their patient. The door was closed. An exiting medical assistant asked them not to enter. He stated that all was good inside, and she was being treated. He stated that he would give them information as he received it.

Braven received a message from the Scout Center that he was needed.

"Braven, you have a responsibility. We have always stressed duty. There is nothing either of us can do right now. Your mother is being taken care of, and I'll keep you informed of her progress. You serve the community, so go serve. We'll be fine."

Braven hesitated. His heart wanted to be there for his mother, but his duty pulled him away. He looked at the triage door. He knew what he needed to do.

"Keep me informed," he reluctantly stated.

"You know I will."

Braven responded to the message and moved toward the exit. He glanced back to see his dad smiling at him. He knew his parents were proud of him.

Braven arrived in the western region. Colonists were hurrying in different directions, some carrying their goods while others assisted the injured. Multiple towers had emerged which defaced the landscape. A congregation of units had been toppled, destroyed, and strewn over the area. Various heaves in the ground gave suspicion that another emergence could happen.

Braven joined another Scout and helped two injured males into a rover for quick transport. Other humanoids jumped inside the vehicle for their escape.

Scouts, military, guards, and volunteers searched for any victims to evacuate the western region of all humanoids. Dozens of uninjured walked while those unable were loaded into hilos and rovers for transport. Soon, the western region was totally cleared.

The rescuers moved to the southern region for the same purpose. Not as many towers emerged there, but there were still too many for comfort.

Braven found a young male who had fallen into a chasm created by one of the monoliths. He retrieved him and asked why he was not with his parents.

The child only stared at Braven's chest and said nothing.

"Are you okay?"

Braven raised the child's chin to look into his face. His eyes were glazed. The male was in shock. Braven carried the child to a rover for medical transport.

Whose child was this? Someone was probably frantically searching for their son. Or maybe they had gotten caught and were on the top of the tower? His mind turned to his own mother.

He checked his messages. Dad had sent one that said his mom's vitals were okay, but she was still unconscious. They were scheduled to leave the planet later today when the physician felt she was stable.

He wanted to see his parents before they left. He knew he would be on the planet for the duration of the evacuation and was not sure when he would meet up with them.

Braven sent a message to the Scout Center to request a break. Having approval, he made his way to see his parents.

Mom was conscious. The lump on her skull gave her

a slight concussion and a tremendous headache. Her left femur was fractured. The physician had just left and told them he had scheduled their immediate medical departure. The family discussed plans to reunite in the space portal and to keep in contact via N-Line and N-View.

"Aren't you both considered essential personnel as department directors?"

"We are, but medical trumps that, and assistant directors will take over if they are needed. Just thinking about it, I don't know if they even need Climatology or Botany Departments right now." Dad had a crooked smile.

Braven laughed. Mom smiled then touched her head and closed her eyes.

The transport arrived. Braven watched as his parents were loaded into the vehicle and were carried away. He watched until they were out of sight. He wanted to join them but had to return to his duties. He returned to the southern region and assisted in recovery.

Section 10

Enlightenment

The day had worn, and Capria was about to disappear. Braven didn't know how long he would be needed or when he would be able to rest. He had not rested for almost two days. His body was tired. His mind was exhausted.

His parents had already left planet, and he was ready to leave as well.

Weston N-Lined that Mesilia delivered her baby. The proud father forwarded a digiphoto of the beautiful female. Chrysila displayed her mother's beautiful skin color yet with more of a lilac hue. She had her father's facial features. Weston said she cried both aloud as well as in the silent Blauken manner.

Braven wanted to see the baby before they departed, but they would probably leave soon. He wondered if Weston would go or stay to help. He wouldn't blame him for leaving.

He sent a request for rest, but it was rejected, and he

was to report to the Scout camp for a special briefing. He stopped and closed his eyes. He didn't remember the last time he had eaten...or slept. He yawned. He rubbed his hands over his face and started toward the camp.

He detoured by the Lounge to take something to eat with him. Upon arriving at Scout camp, he could see numerous rovers on their way to the air portal. *Where are those coming from? The southern and western regions are almost cleared.*

He hurried to the conference room for the special briefing. The room was crowded with military personnel, Scouts, colony leaders, and scientists.

"Alpha evacuations are on schedule. The other colonies have been contacted about the events. Evacuations are happening at all sites due to the invasion of monoliths. Kappa colonists arrived this morning. Gamma should be here any time. We have word that Iota Colony had been overrun with monoliths, and we lost contact. General Artula dispatched military to the area. We hope to hear something soon." Director Fortuna paused. "You are all doing a fine job. Continue your work."

He turned to Scout Archer.

"As for our Scout staff, Scout Hastern will be evacuating with his spouse and newborn daughter today."

Braven looked around. He hadn't seen Weston nor heard that news. He was happy for them and would catch up with them at the space portal and meet his beautiful daughter.

"Some of you haven't slept in a day or more. Scout Able will be coordinating shifts so everyone can get a little rest. Please see him after this meeting."

The Scout nodded at Dr. Valtera, the interplanetary zoologist.

"It seems we have a new species in the universe. This species of flora abides underground on this planet and uses tentacles, which we know as monoliths, for nourishment. For years, it was thought that the monoliths were just granite or gabbro rock, but we have discovered that when a tentacle dies, or possibly becomes dormant, it solidifies to a rock-like substance. The monoliths are somehow related to a central processor we refer to as the 'Mother,' are produced through spore production called monokaryotic mycelia, and spread through stolons. In layman's terms, the monoliths are all connected through a central nervous system that spreads all over this planet."

Wait, that's what Mom was talking about.

"Now, the problem we may be encountering soon is the harvest. Each one of these monoliths carries an infant caprodome."

Gasps erupted in the silent crowd.

Braven could not believe what he was hearing. *Those things would annihilate all humanoid life.*

"Through DNA analysis, it has been determined that the monoliths and the caprodomes have the same DNA structure. This is an incredible find to the scientific world since we have discovered a creature that not only has flora and fauna characteristics but is both flora and fauna.

"Because of this influx of infant caprodomes, we must ensure the safety of all colonists and yourselves. We know that the creatures do not go into the light, so after Capria sets, all lights must be illuminated, and humanoids remain inside. General."

The general turned to the doctor.

"Thank you, Dr. Valtera. We have discovered the probable reason for this invasion. Years earlier, Zeta Colony was established near a mining camp. The mining process used explosives to clear ground and harvest. Blasts from the mine caused the behemoth to awaken from its dormant state. Monoliths were in the Zeta area but not active. During the ground movement caused by the blasts, it is believed that the 'Mother' was alerted to life and activated there for nourishment. Since the clearing of the colony and camp, the spread stopped. When Alpha began major expansion toward the southern and western regions last year, more explosives were used. The creature must have sensed the vibrations that alerted it to its food source. It reproduced to actively pursue the humanoids for nourishment with the help of their offspring, the caprodomes."

Braven was glad his parents were off planet. He was glad Weston and Mesilia were leaving. Knowing more about the dangers of those creatures was not comforting.

After the meeting, Braven approached Scout Able for his assignment schedule. The senior Scout was aware of his overdue rest period, so he was released until next shift. Braven was glad and retreated to his unit.

He N-Viewed his parents. They were doing fine and awaiting his arrival. He sent a message to Weston. They had just arrived at the air portal and were looking for the Tritons. He said he would N-Line him as soon as he got settled.

***

Braven awoke after falling out of his sleeper. The ground shook violently for only a few seconds. He was afraid to move. He assessed the environment.

The unit was intact with no visible damage. He was uninjured. Capria was still shining but at dusk. He slowly got up, and as he opened the front door, he could see a monolith had emerged and virtually blocked his exit. He scurried to the back window and escaped. The two units in front of his had been damaged. Fortunately, those Scouts were on duty and not in their units.

He moved toward the Scout camp. Besides the new monolith at his unit, there was another just to the south.

Armed military and guards were lining the roadways and perimeter. Braven was thankful they were present.

As he entered the camp, he was informed by a passerby that a caprodome had been seen.

"When?"

"About two hours ago."

"There's no way. Caprodomes don't come out during the daylight."

The commenter just shrugged.

That must be a rumor. But if it's true, then we are in big trouble.

Braven hurried to the Scout headquarters. He reported the newly erupted monolith and asked about the reported caprodome.

"We know nothing about that."

A sense of relief blanketed him. He readied himself for his shift. He added a stun pistol as an additional protection device...just in case.

On patrol, Timlo joined Braven. They patrolled the area around the air portal. A perimeter fence had been erected since he had last been there. A new fencing method was established which was buried deep within the ground.

Hopefully, that will keep the portal safe.

Colonists from Gamma had arrived and awaited their transport. Most non-essential colonists from Alpha had been evacuated. The remainder of Kappa colonists left on the last evac. There was still no word on Iota Colony. A hilo had been sent out to visibly check on the colony. Nighttime flights had been cancelled, so Braven knew if they had not already left, a hilo would depart when Capria rose to find any stragglers.

The normal serenity after dark was no more. Colonists in the portal perimeter chattered, and vehicles passed by routinely. High alert was issued to watch skyward for any unusual movement. Braven was careful to always keep his back against something. He did not want any surprises.

Braven and Timlo walked along the perimeter. Their eyes moved continually with their heads raised. Braven had his power light and stun pistol handy. He shared with Timlo the dangers of caprodomes and a little of his experience with them. He tried to stay away from the emotion of it all.

Hours passed. Braven and Timlo talked. Mainly Braven talked. Timlo's quiet disposition was a distinguishing characteristic, but Braven felt awkward at times.

During a time of quiet, Braven heard a faintly familiar, yet definite noise. He froze and stared in that direction.

It can't be.

He swallowed hard. His upward search alerted

Timlo of danger.

"What's going on?" Timlo quietly asked.

"Listen," Braven whispered and held his hand out palm down.

Quiet.

"What did you hear?"

"Shh."

Quiet.

Timlo looked at his databoard. A message appeared that stated:

High Alert: caprodomes have been spotted in the central region. Remain in the light and report any sighting.

"Braven."

Braven stood quietly.

Timlo placed his hand on his partner's shoulder and repeated, "Braven."

The young Scout slowly looked at his companion.

"Timlo, I just heard a caprodome."

Section 11

Marooned

The exterior of the air portal was well-lit. There was no concern for the creature to invade that area. Streets and perimeters were illuminated. Buildings were surrounded with light. Caprodomes would be deterred from most of the colony.

Braven made sure to stay under one of the bright perimeter lights as they patrolled the boundary. He warned Timlo of being too slow to get under one of the lights. He constantly viewed the dark sky for any signs of movement.

The night dragged on until finally a hint of light illuminated the distant western horizon. The tensity in Braven's body dissipated as he saw the gradual daylight make its way into the sky. As he relaxed, his energy waned. He could barely keep his eyes open. His shift ended, and he found a room at the Scout camp to rest.

*****

Braven awoke and opened the door to see shuffling

in the hallway. It was midmorning. All shifts had been cancelled, and all remaining humanoids were required to work until they were evacuated.

Timlo, Rimi, and Braven made up Scout Able's team. They were dispatched for a final search of any stranded humanoids in the eastern region. They piled into a rover and headed out.

On the way, Braven was saddened by the discovery that Iota Colony had been destroyed by monoliths, and the final search for humanoids came up empty. The last of the Gamma colonists had evacuated, and there was only one more transport for all non-essential personnel to be evacuated. Then, the last of the humanoids would depart.

Finally, now we can all leave this planet.

Scout Able parked the vehicle in the center of the region. He took Timlo and paired Rimi and Braven to do a quick patrol of the area before moving on.

Braven and Rimi searched inside houses, looked in windows, and circled every unit. They passed a monolith and beelined for the next unit cluster. Section after section they traveled and stayed alert for any signs of life while they kept in constant communication with Scout Able.

They continued their search in the clusters of units. One would enter a unit while the other circled it. They patterned their search, so they didn't return to any one unit or cluster. The last cluster in their section was ahead.

They received word that they should return to the camp within two hours for evacuation.

"That will be enough time to get away from this place before those winged creatures come to eat anyone," Braven said in relief.

"I'm not looking to be here to see that." Rimi scoured the sky for the creatures.

Braven could see that his tales of the caprodome unnerved his friend.

He went inside the first unit of the cluster while Rimi circled the exterior. A rumble under the surface caught them both off guard.

"Let's hurry and get out of here." Braven walked around the inside of the unit. He stopped in the front room and took out his databoard to report the tremblor.

An explosion under the unit hurled dirt, dust, and the unit into the air. The unit detonated. Braven went airborne.

***

Braven slowly opened his eyes. He was face down. He was covered in debris, and a thick layer of dust was chokingly thick. Something large and heavy covered his head and torso. Extreme pain radiated in his left side and chest. It was hard to breathe. He felt pain in his head, chest, left arm, and hand. He groaned. He tried to get up but was unsuccessful. The large object was straddling his back and kept him bound to the surface. He didn't have the strength to move out from under whatever it was. He lay there silently for a few minutes before he called for help.

"Rimi."

Quiet.

"Rimi, I'm over here."

Still no response.

He coughed. His side hurt. The dust was choking, and he could hardly cough because of the pain. The smell was horrible.

He managed to push the debris off his head. He turned to his right to see that he was outside but was not on the ground. He couldn't determine what was beneath him. He looked in other directions. Nothing different. Everything was dingy like it was dusk. *Why is Capria not shining? It's early afternoon. Probably because this dust is too thick.*

He laid his head on his right hand. *Assess, Braven.*

Am I in danger? Hmm. I don't even know where I am.

Be cautious of what could happen. Lying on my stomach with something on top of my back pinning me down. Pain in my chest and side. Vulnerable right now.

Know my surroundings. On top of something. Looks dusk to dark. But it can't be dark already. Was I knocked out? How long have I been here?

Consider what to do.

"Well, I'm in a bad situation," Braven spoke verbally.

He called for his fellow Scout again. No response.

He gathered his strength and pushed himself up enough to turn on his side. The pain was excruciating. He yelled loudly.

Finally, on his back, he used his uninjured arm and slightly lifted the object enough to slowly move himself out from underneath. He lay there for a moment holding in his pain.

Slowly raising up to view his surroundings, Braven noticed that he was on top of a structure. He must have been propelled by the eruption to the top of a unit. There was a unit toppled between where he lay and the monolith. He must have been flung high through the air.

He got more understanding of the area. It was getting darker. Where was his team.

"Rimi?"

"Timlo?"

"Able?"

"Anyone?"

Each name grew louder as desperation set in.

Where is everyone? A blanket of hopelessness covered the young man.

It was late morning when we came out. I remember the tremblor happening and I got my databoard...

"My databoard." He searched the area where he had awoken. He looked all over the roof for it. He looked at the ground and all around the unit. Nothing.

He searched his pockets and only found the stun pistol. Nothing else. His power light was missing. *At least I have something.*

He scanned the roof and alongside the unit to find a way to the ground. He could jump, but with his ribs possibly broken, that would be much too painful.

He found a wallboard from the toppled unit that leaned against the structure where he was. He carefully made his way down the outside of the building until he hit the ground, taking his breath. Pain shot through his body. He bent for a few minutes holding his left side.

He finally rose to see a darkening sky.

Light. I've got to find some light.

He searched the area. No light to be found.

Where is the perimeter lighting? Or the streetlamps?

He decided to make his way back to the Scout camp to join the others. He would have to travel as stealthily as possible. He didn't want any encounter with a flying monster.

He slowly made his way through the eastern region nearing the Central Commons. He stopped at times to gain his composure. His breathing was very labored. As he arrived, he saw no lights anywhere.

What is going on?

The sky was dark. Capria was gone. Wilstor and Kadyen were nowhere in sight.

Why did tonight have to be the darkest night in this planet's history?

He knew he needed to somehow reach the Scout Comm Center, but the darkness overtook him. He needed a place to shelter.

They wouldn't leave me here, would they? A streak of anxiety flickered through his body.

He turned toward the medical building. It was still basically undamaged by the monolith eruptions. Maybe he could find someone, some communications equipment, or at least pain reduction inside.

The lighting in the building had been disabled as it had been in the streets. The electronic doors remained closed as he approached. He pulled them open for entry but made sure they were closed after him to keep everything out. He entered the first room on the right and found a closet in the back. He opened the door but couldn't see what was inside. He felt his way inside until he could close the door. He left the door open a few centimeters to hear or see anything coming close.

He sat quietly. His breathing slowed and his pain dulled a bit. Hours dragged by and sleep overtook him. He awoke enough to realize he needed to close the door in case something tried to get inside the room. As he reached to close the door, he could hear the yips of caprodomes around the building. He slowly took the handle and eased the door closed. He sat for hours without sleep and heard disturbing sounds in the distance.

He reassured himself that he was safe, and Capria would rise soon. He thought of his parents, where they were, and how they were doing at the space portal. Where would all the colonists go since evacuating Jedira? How soon would they depart? Would Jedira be vacant of humanoid life forever? Would his parents be sent to another planet, and he not see them for years?

Happy thoughts, Braven! His parents taught him that when he constantly dwelled on negative thoughts, they caused anxiety and fear. Braven had always tried to keep his thoughts positive.

He thought of his friends from the Academy. He wondered where they were and what adventures they had experienced. He wondered where his childhood friends were. He hadn't heard what happened to Khara. Was she evacuated safely?

Khara. Braven smiled. She nursed him back to health when he was almost dead. Khara, who spoke so bravely and wisely at the exact time when it was needed. Khara, whose company Braven enjoyed when the Twins were such a pain to him.

I think I could like her. I need to N-Line her again.

A noise banged in the room outside the closet door. Braven stopped breathing. His thoughts fled as sweat began to bead on his brow.

He slowly reached for his stun pistol.

A yip sounded in the distance.

That wasn't inside the room?

He listened intently. He closed his eyes and continued shallow breaths.

Did they get in? Are they leaving?

Braven wanted to open the door to check but knew that was not wise. He sat quietly.

After another hour, Braven heard a sliding noise. He raised his head. He held his ear to the door to hear anything else. Nothing.

He wondered if Capria had appeared or if it was still dark outside. He wanted to open the door for a visual. Since losing his databoard, he had no sense of time while in the closet. He waited a little longer. No sound.

Finally, he reached for the handle and quietly unlatched it. He moved close to the opening so he could see more clearly. Light illuminated through the windows. Capria had risen. He could see the details of the room. It was one of the few exam rooms at the colony. He could see the table and where the machines were once connected.

He slowly opened the door further to see that it was a small room of only a few meters square. As he opened the door even more, it was hindered. He held up his stun pistol and started closing the door. A humanoid hand grabbed the door and swung it open.

Braven instinctively flared the pistol. The hand disappeared.

"Hello." An unfamiliar voice sounded.

Braven struggled to stand. He strained his injured ribs and slunk back into the closet. He held his side and released a quiet groan.

"Who's there?"

"I'm Keyloi Gravton."

Braven was relieved. "Braven Triton. I'm a Scout."

A head popped around the door. "Really?"

Braven and the young, ruddy-skinned male stared at each other for a moment. The youth looked about thirteen years old with red hair that matched his freckles. He was small in stature with captivatingly green eyes.

"I didn't know you were in there. I've been here most of the night trying to stay away from the caprodomes." The excitement in his voice was evidence that he was thrilled to find another humanoid.

"Where are the others?" Braven asked after a groan.

"They've all gone. I saw the last shuttle flying away yesterday but didn't know where to go. I'm glad I found you. How soon can we leave?"

Braven struggled to get up; the boy helped. His small frame was stronger than Braven thought. Braven grunted. Pain shot through his left side.

"Are you okay?"

"I'll be fine. You saw the last shuttle? How do you know it was the last?"

"I went to the air portal. No one was there, and all of the shuttles were gone."

Braven thought of how that could have happened. He woke up alone, and it was getting dark. The team he was with had left for the eastern region late that morning. Why would they have left him? And how did the young male get left?

"Why are you still here?"

"Long story," Braven grunted. "I'll explain later."

"What are we going to do?"

"Listen." Braven tried to hamper the boy's excitement. "I'm hurting and need something for the pain, and I haven't eaten in a while. I'm going to see if I can find something while we're here and then go to the Lounge."

"I can help with the pain. Wait here." With a snap, Keyloi was out the door.

Braven wasn't sure what to expect since the adolescent left without explanation. He made his way over to the exam table for support and stood quietly.

Within a few minutes, the young humanoid returned with a dispenser. "Here's a dose of dologra. It's a pain killer."

Braven looked at the contraption and then at the boy. "Where did you get that, and how do you know what to get?"

"My dad is a physician. This was his room. I've been his intern this last year." A sense of accomplishment covered the young teen's countenance. "Do you want me to administer it?"

Surprised by the recent discovery, Braven agreed. The youth dispensed the pain reliever, and, within minutes, Braven's pain diminished.

"That will last for twelve to fifteen hours."

"Well, aren't you handy to have around?"

"You just say it because it's true." A grin came over the boy's face.

Braven's mind wandered to his friends who used that phrase with each other. He smiled.

Keyloi examined the area of Braven's pain. "Probably broken ribs. If my dad was here, he could just repair your bones, but they took the machine. Do you have problems breathing?"

Braven nodded.

"You will need some more dologra in the next couple of days. I know where it is kept when you need some more."

Braven was amazed at the confidence in the youth. It reminded him of his young friend, Skylar, the walking scientific database.

The two made their way to the Lounge for nourishment. Inside, everything was gone. They searched the cabinets and storage rooms. Nothing.

"Everyone has been packing everything for the evac. I think I know where we can find something."

The youth led Braven back to the medical facility and down the hallway to a room at the end. There was a breakroom that still had a few food packets left.

"I noticed these yesterday afternoon after the last shuttle. They may have just missed it or run out of time and didn't clean it all out. The same for the dologra. There was an entire cabinet of medicines left."

"Good break for us." Braven dove into one of the packaged meals. "By the way, why are you still here?"

The boy explained that he was to be on the second to last shuttle, but his dad was scheduled for the last shuttle. He wanted to stay with him, but his dad was absolute about his going on to be safe. He sent him a message that he was safe and would see him later, but he hid out for the next shuttle so he could leave with his dad. He fell asleep, and by the time he awoke, the last shuttle had taken off.

"I'm glad I found you. I don't know what to do."

"We'll stay together and figure this out. You sure you

haven't seen anyone else?"

"Not yet, but I haven't moved around the colony much."

After they both took nourishment, they headed toward the Scout camp. Braven knew he could find something, or maybe someone, at the Comm Center.

As they arrived, it was obvious that the ground had swollen underneath the structure. There was no monolith present, but it looked similar to other places where the ground erupted with one. They observed the scene for a moment and then backed away.

Braven stopped his companion.

"Do you have a databoard?"

"I'm only twelve. My dad said the rules are fourteen."

"He's right about that. Do you know where there may be any electronics anywhere?"

He thought for a moment. "No."

"We must get word to the space portal that we are still here. I lost my databoard, and we can't get into the Comm Center. The admin building was destroyed."

The boy said nothing. Braven felt lost.

"Let's look around and see if we can find any type of communications device. In an emergency evac, someone had to have left something." Braven was trying to inspire hope, mainly in himself.

They went to the air portal, but a monolith stood where the space shuttle pad was and another stood outside the building.

"That's probably not a good place to go. Let's try the Commons."

The two began their search in all public structures—the section of the admin building that was unaffected, the med center, the research labs, the instruction center, and the Lounge. Nothing. They went to individual units. Nothing.

Everyone was very thorough in their departure. No electronic equipment of any kind was found. They found personal effects in every unit. Some units were disheveled, and others were pristine. Still no luck.

Their search continued throughout the day. No communication devices were found. Keyloi found a small power light.

"Great find. Keep that with you. Caps don't like the light."

The youth was proud of his discovery.

After the day was spent, they made their way back to the medical center. They searched for rooms with no windows and two doors in case they had to escape. None were found. All had either windows or only one door. They decided on no windows.

The room they found was a relieving room with one

door, no windows, and a relief station. There was room enough for both to rest. They had no way to know the time except Capria's position in the sky, so they would need to occasionally look for any light coming through the windows outside their hideaway.

They gathered food items, various cloth items for beds, a couple of medical doses, and returned to their lair as darkness overtook them. They sat and quietly talked.

"Where is your planet?"

"I was born on Radzier. Couldn't you tell by my handsome complexion?" The boy giggled.

Braven smiled. "I didn't take you for a Blauken. By the way, how do Radzierians distinguish the name of the planet from the name of the star?"

"That's always a problem for outsiders. The star is pronounced Radzier, but the planet is Radzier."

"That sounds the same to me." Braven gave a crooked smile.

The boy articulated the names. The slight intonation of his pronunciation could have been easily missed if he hadn't pointed it out.

"I hear the difference. I've always relied on context clues."

They talked for a short while. Braven asked him if he could stay awake for a little while as he napped. He was going to take either shift the boy did not want. The boy agreed to stay awake for the first shift. Braven told him that when he started getting too sleepy, to wake him and he would take the rest of the night. The youth agreed.

Braven lay on his makeshift bed. The room was small but still comfortable enough for them both. Keyloi stayed attentive for any noise and made sure the door stayed closed.

***

Braven opened his eyes. He could hear the caprodomes outside the building. They did not sound as if they were inside the exterior room.

"Keyloi?" Braven whispered.

No answer.

Braven reached where the boy was sitting and felt his shoulder. He was sleeping. Braven hadn't slept too well that night. The surface was uncomfortable, and a dull pain in his ribs kept him from turning. He stayed awake for the rest of the night. He was glad Keyloi could get some rest.

Braven sat up and leaned against the wall. He wondered what time it was and how long he had been sleeping. He didn't blame Keyloi for napping. After all, he was only twelve. Maybe they could sleep some during the daytime.

He sat quietly and listened to the occasional call from the monsters. His mind drifted to his friends and parents. His Academy buddies were discovering the universe, and there he was hiding from monsters. His parents probably grieved since they lost their only child...again. Weston and Mesilia enjoyed their new baby. Where was Khara's destination?

His thoughts turned to Keyloi. His father was a physician and probably grieved over the loss of his son. Did he have his mother with him? He had only mentioned his dad. Does his father even realize that Keyloi was left?

Hours later, the raucous noises of the caprodomes diminished. Braven felt Capria was about to rise, so it would be good for them to exit and search for some way to escape the planet.

He tapped his companion on the foot to awaken him. The youth stirred. He sat up and asked what time it was.

"It's morning. Let's get started on searching units to the east."

Braven's pain steadily returned. Breathing deeply grew difficult. He stopped to nurture his side.

He slowly unlatched the door handle and carefully eased the door open. A sliver of light broke the deep darkness of the room. He felt relieved.

Braven swung the door open to reveal a caprodome staring at him.

Section 12

The Visitor

Braven slammed the door. Keyloi retreated to the rear wall. Braven held the handle tightly.

"It's daytime!" Keyloi strongly whispered. "Why is that thing still outside?"

"Get out your power light."

The boy fumbled in his pockets and dropped the light on the floor. He searched around to retrieve it. He hunkered against the back wall with the light shining on the door.

Braven held tightly to the handle. He reached for his stun pistol and readied it.

The terror on the face of the young male was a picture of fear itself. His eyes bulged and sweat beads appeared. He whimpered and hyperventilated.

Braven mouthed the words "it's okay" as calmly as he could. "Breathe!" he whispered, disguising his own terror.

There was a harsh scraping sound outside the door. Silence. Braven waited. He put his ear to the door. He heard nothing. He looked at Keyloi.

"Why would it be in the light? That doesn't make sense," Braven whispered silently, almost as if only moving his lips.

Keyloi held his ground. He didn't respond but just stared at the Scout.

They waited another half hour. Still silent outside the door.

Braven slowly moved toward the door. "I'm going to check if it's still out there."

"Don't open it," Keyloi pleaded as he shook his head.

"It must be gone. I don't hear anything." Braven waited another five minutes. "If it's still there, I'll use my stun pistol."

This seemed to calm the youth a bit. He kept his power light directed at the door.

Braven slowly opened the door with a watchful eye. He searched as much of the room as he could in all directions as the door opened. He listened for any evidence of the creature. Nothing.

He slowly opened the door until he could exit, always keeping alert. He motioned for Keyloi. Hesitantly, the youth exited the room and hurried to the Scout's side.

Braven held his fingertips to his lips to sign for

quiet. He made his way to exit into the hallway. The youth remained on his heels.

As he opened the door to the hallway, Braven could see large items lumped on the floor all along the long, dark passageway. He looked closer. He took Keyloi's power light to see better.

He backed up and crowded the young male before quickly closing the door.

"There may be a dozen caprodomes in the hallway," he quietly whispered.

Concern flooded Keyloi's composure.

Braven touched his arm and told him to breathe. He realized he was teaching him the same techniques that Weston taught him at Zeta Colony.

"Why are they here?"

Braven thought for a moment. "They need a dark place to rest during the day. The dark hallway with no windows would be a perfect place for them." Braven had a revelation. He then knew where they stayed during the light of day. They needed to avoid those places.

They opened one of the windows in the room and peered out. The boy leaped outside. Braven tried to get out the window, but his chest pain grew steadily. He tried to raise himself, but the pain grew.

Keyloi watched his new friend. He climbed back inside and knelt on his hands and knees in front of the window.

"Step on my back to get out."

"I'm too heavy for you."

"Do it. We need to get out of here."

Braven braced himself and stepped on the boy's lower back and hips. He pulled himself up enough to exit the window. He landed on his feet outside the window and a pain shot through his chest. He let out a quiet groan. As quickly as Braven touched the ground, the boy followed.

"You need another dose." The youth returned inside the window before Braven could respond. He quickly returned with the medicine and food packets. He administered a dose of the pain-relieving medication.

"Amazing how quickly that works." Braven inhaled deeply but then coughed and grabbed his side.

"Don't overdo it."

Braven winced and agreed.

The pair decided to walk toward the air portal. Keyloi chatted as Braven surveyed the area. He could see the destruction the monoliths had caused. He knew the caprodomes were out during the night, but they couldn't be successful in finding food unless they ate flora.

As they arrived outside the portal's perimeter, they observed the monolith that destroyed the shuttle pad. How would a shuttle land without its pad? That pad was constructed specifically for the air shuttle. Without the pad, the shuttle might settle on softer soil and become unstable.

"Could it get any worse?" the boy sighed.

A small groundquake happened. No eruptions. No monoliths appeared.

With wide eyes, Keyloi continued, "I won't ask that anymore."

Braven chuckled. Even though he was lighthearted on the outside, Braven was very concerned about what they would do, if they would be rescued, and how they would survive since the monsters invaded.

"Well," Braven thought out loud.

"Well, what?"

"Oh, I was just thinking about what we need to do next. It doesn't look like an air shuttle will be coming, and without communications, we don't know when anyone will come to rescue us."

"So, what about the caprodomes?"

"They'll come around at night, so we will make sure we are somewhere safe before Capria sets."

"You mean we won't be leaving?"

"Not right now. Maybe the military will send a Scouting drone to check things out."

"Why can't they send a hilo?"

"From space?"

"Oh, yeah." The youngster's face reddened even deeper.

"It's okay. We'll figure something out. Just stay near me, and if you see anything out of the norm, let me know."

Keyloi chuckled. "Um, there are a lot of things out of the norm."

Braven laughed aloud. "You are so right." The pair shared a time of laughter.

Braven knew they were in grave danger, but he did not want his young friend to sense his fear. With the shuttle pad destroyed, there was no safe way for an air shuttle to land. He thought there must be some way since someone built the pad in the first place. Safe shelter would be tough to find since the caprodomes invaded the buildings each night. Food had been evacuated by the colonists. Braven knew he could find water with the night mists, but they could not survive without food for very long. Their future looked dismal, but he had always been a positive survivor. At least his mother said so.

The dull pain in his chest and side gradually returned. He mentioned to Keyloi about getting more medicine for later.

"I'm not going back in that building." Keyloi threw his hands up in front of him.

"Okay, but will you tell me where you found it?"

"You won't make it without me."

"Why not?"

"I'll have to show you."

"Let's go then."

Keyloi hesitated. He had a look of strain as he thought of re-entering the building. Braven felt he was pulled between the new inhabitants versus his pain management.

"Just tell me what room it's in."

Keyloi was reluctant then sighed. "Let's go. While we are there, we need to clear out the food locker. I don't want to go back in there with them." It looked like the youngster dropped a fifty-kilogram sack from his back as he made the decision to return with Braven.

"Good thinking." Braven was proud of his young friend for making a tough decision. He thought it was very mature of him.

The duo returned to the medical building and looked through a window. Keyloi moved to the next window, and the next, until he found the intended room.

"There it is." He pointed to some closet doors and a set of cabinets.

Braven tried the window, but it was immovable.

"Can you just break it?"

"Windows don't break. Unless the building is toppled by a monolith."

Keyloi giggled.

Braven looked to see Capria still high in the sky. He asked his friend to move back. He took his stun pistol and smashed at the bottom corner of the window. Nothing. He hit it again. Nothing.

"So, how can we get in?"

Braven could not imagine tiptoeing through the midst of sleeping caprodomes. He shuddered at the thought.

"I don't know."

He walked to the end of the building to peer down the hallway. With Keyloi's power light, he could count seven or eight lumps on the floor. Each looked as if they were about half his size; not nearly as large as the one he had encountered at Zeta.

They look so small, like baby caprodomes. I wonder how much they could eat. I wonder what they eat.

Braven had never thought of the diet of the caprodome. He assumed it was humanoids, but what about when there were no humanoids around? They must eat something.

"We cannot get to the meds or that food right now. We need to plan a time to get it. We still have one dose with us so it can wait until tomorrow morning. Let's continue our search for food and communications equipment."

Keyloi agreed. They headed toward the western region to check in nearby buildings. They didn't want to venture too far away if they couldn't find a safe shelter.

After visiting two dozen empty units with no success,

they returned to the Commons. They discussed a safe shelter for the night. Both had thoughts, but neither was sure their place was safe enough.

They meandered around the structures and sought some room without windows but with an exterior door so the creatures wouldn't block it while they slept. After a pointed search, they came across an entrance into the educational building that opened into a mechanical room. There was a door that entered the hallway. There were no windows and plenty of room for them both to stretch out to rest.

"Perfect!" Braven exclaimed. "Now we need to fortify it."

By that time, Braven had severe pain in his lower side and chest. He found a place to rest and caress his side. His breathing grew labored.

"Why am I hurting so soon? You gave me the pain relief earlier this morning." Braven held his side.

"Hey, rest a minute. I'll be back." At that, the youth took off running.

"Wait. Where are you going?"

The boy didn't look back.

Braven sat quietly. He managed his breathing and held his torso. He closed his eyes and faced the sky. Capria's warmth felt nice. He remained there for a few minutes until he heard a distant noise. He opened his eyes.

That couldn't be what I think it is?

He lowered his head and slowly turned to his right. Nothing. He turned to his left. Still nothing.

What was that noise? His mind wondered what would even make noise.

That had to be Keyloi. But it didn't sound like Keyloi.

He heard it again behind him at a far distance. He slowly rotated his body. He saw nothing out of the normal.

Keyloi, you need to get back here.

Another sound.

What is going on? Braven slowly stood through the pain and saw a very small creature wobbling along toward him. He stood in wonder. He had never seen a creature like that.

Is that a caprodome? It looks like one but somewhat different.

Braven was captivated by the creature. Small—about forty centimeters tall with light brown fur on its body but none on its head. Four legs, a tail, and a long neck. It had a few characteristics of a caprodome, but many more dissimilar.

The tiny fauna scampered right up to Braven and made a circle around his left leg. Braven just stood there in shock. He had never seen anything like this.

Where did this come from? It can't be a caprodome

because Capria's light doesn't bother it. There are no other creatures on planet so what is this?

The animal rolled on its back and kicked its four feet playfully as it returned to standing. Braven just stood and watched. He didn't know how to respond. He quickly looked around the area for any danger. No other creature was nearby. He was afraid to touch it in case it had a disease or would attack him. He just stood still.

The creature rolled on the ground, jumped, spun in circles, sat, looked at him, and made a tiny squeaking sound. It rubbed its head on Braven's leg.

Braven surveyed his surroundings again. *Something's not right. Where has this creature been all these years, and why is it out now?*

Braven saw Keyloi coming from a distance. He was carrying something as he ran. "Whoa, what's that?"

Braven looked at the male and slowly responded, "I'm not sure."

Keyloi placed his goods on the ground and approached the beast. It wobbled to him and snuggled against his leg.

"It's friendly. Where did it come from?" Keyloi bent down to play with it.

"That way." Braven pointed toward the western region. "I'm not sure you should be playing with it. We don't know what it is or its origin."

"It's like a limya from my planet. They are playful, and some humanoids keep them for comfort and play. This doesn't look exactly like a limya, but it acts like it."

"But how did it get here? And why is it just now showing up?" Braven surveyed the area once again. He felt something was amiss.

"Oh, I got some more meds for you."

"Why am I hurting so soon? The last doses helped all day."

"This morning's dose may have been smaller. This one is for twelve hours."

Keyloi opened and administered the painkiller to the Scout. Within minutes, Braven felt the relief start.

"And I got some nourishment."

Braven looked at the boy and asked where he got it.

"Uh, I found a way into the room."

"Keyloi! You can't just run off like that without at least letting me know where you're going. You can't get around those sleeping creatures. We must be a team if we're going to survive."

The youth looked chastised. "I'm sorry." He returned to playing with the fauna.

"We need to prepare our shelter for the night. Capria will be disappearing soon."

The two returned to their lair and stored the items inside. The little limya followed in its playful manner.

Braven checked his stun pistol and Keyloi's power light.

As Capria set and dusk settled in, the pair made their way inside. The limya stood outside the door. Keyloi coaxed it in, but it refused to enter and only squeaked.

"Why won't it come in?"

Suddenly, the small creature took off running.

"Limya! Limya! Where is he going? We can't leave it outside tonight."

Braven grabbed the boy's arm as he was about to run after it.

"That thing has a safe place because the caprodomes haven't found it yet. Let it go for tonight, and we'll see what happens in the morning."

"No, it needs our help."

"No, it does not. We tried, but it took off. I would rather the caps eat that thing rather than you or me."

"No, it won't survive."

"It has this far. It knows what it's doing. It has been safe for its whole life. We will probably see it in the morning."

At that, Keyloi calmed down, and Braven secured both doors.

Section 13

Traitor

The night was quiet. Keyloi laid with his back to Braven. He was upset that the limya didn't stay and that Braven would not allow him to go after it. Braven tried to converse but received no response. He told Keyloi to get some rest. The youth did not move.

So how can I talk with an angry preteen when he's upset, angry at me, and not interested in talking? Does he treat his dad this way? Was I wrong in letting the limya go? It will probably be eaten tonight. But there was no way I was going to let him take off after it when it was getting dark. He would have been eaten, too. Some day he will understand logic.

It was quiet. The caprodomes had not stirred. Braven pondered where Keyloi and he would work in the morning. They needed to communicate with the space portal somehow about them still being on planet. But how could they do that without any equipment?

Braven heard a quiet noise. He raised his head. That wasn't the sound of a caprodome. There it was again.

Keyloi stirred.

The noise was louder. It was a squeak that sounded like the small creature.

"Is that the limya?"

"Quiet," Braven whispered.

The noise grew until it sounded outside their door.

"It is the limya." Keyloi jumped up and moved to the door.

Braven grabbed the boy's arm. "You are not opening that door."

"But the limya is outside. It needs us to protect it."

The squeaking continued.

"You can't let the limya get killed." He reached for the door handle.

Braven grabbed his arm.

"We are not opening that door. Capria is gone, and the caprodomes are ready to go out."

"I don't hear any caprodomes, but I hear the limya pleading for help."

Braven thought. *If the limya is alone, it would be a target for the caps. The caps may not be active yet. We could reach out, grab the limya, and secure the door. It shouldn't take that long.*

Braven listened intently. The squeaking continued.

"I'll check to see if it's okay." Braven relented. "Any sign of danger, this door closes and will not be opened. Agree?"

Keyloi responded positively.

Braven took his stun pistol in one hand and held the doorknob with the other. His breathing increased; his heart pounded. The squeaking beckoned him. Keyloi illuminated his power light.

Braven slowly unlatched the door and opened it a few centimeters. He saw nothing. He heard the squeaks behind the door. He needed to open wider. He carefully increased the opening enough to reveal the limya. He held out his hand to coax it to him.

Suddenly, a rushing snap hit his hand but did not grasp it. A caprodome shot at the door, but Braven slammed it. He held the handle stiff while the monster pounded on the door.

Keyloi screamed.

"Quiet!" Braven strongly whispered.

The pounding increased. The number of loud yips expanded to include several creatures. Braven held on tightly in case the exterior handle was broken.

Keyloi hunkered at the interior door. It was locked and the farthest position away from the creatures. Braven maintained his position as the creatures pounded on the exterior door. The door was locked, but Braven wanted no accidental opening.

The hammering continued seemingly for hours. Braven continued holding the handle and could see it was still locked. He kept his grip solid.

"What happened to the limya?" Keyloi asked.

"The limya was decoy. It was working with the caprodomes."

"I don't understand."

"The limya survives the daylight to Scout for suspected victims and then brings the caprodomes at night."

"I didn't know. I almost got us killed."

"We are alive, and I mean to keep it that way."

Pounding began on the interior door. Keyloi jumped at Braven.

"Hold that handle, and do not let it unlock."

The youth hesitated.

"Get that handle now. We need to hold them off."

Keyloi went back to the door and grabbed the handle as directed.

"They know we're in here and are adamant about getting to us. We need to hold them off until Capria rises."

"How long will that be?"

"Who knows? We'll wait until these guys are tired and all the pounding stops."

Hours passed. The two still held their door handles

but with less tensity. The constant stress tired the two, but they held on.

The pounding slowed. It sounded as though only one creature pounded each door rather than the multitude. The yips were less frequent. Soon, the hammering ceased.

It was quiet.

Braven told the lad that they could release the handles but make sure they remained locked. It looked like Capria might be rising. They sat back and relaxed. Keyloi shook and stretched his hands. Braven could feel the tightness in his shoulders. They both needed to rest.

"I can't believe the limya was part of it."

"I can't believe the creatures were able to strategize that way." Braven was baffled at their ability to work together.

"What do the caprodomes eat? If they only eat humanoids or other fauna, there are none on this planet. Well, except you and me." Keyloi stated with apprehension.

Braven chuckled. "That's a question no one can answer. They may be omnivores and use flora as nourishment as well. No one has been able to study them. Why don't we just rest rather than leave the room. We need to get some sleep."

At that, the two stretched out and fell fast asleep.

***

Braven opened his eyes. His chest and side were in

pain. His shoulders and hands ached. He groaned.

He turned on the power light. Keyloi was still asleep. He approached the exterior door and slowly opened it. Capria's light flooded the room. Relief flooded him.

He stepped outside to see Capria was at midmorning.

We didn't sleep very long. Or maybe the caprodomes left us alone early. I really wish I had my databoard.

Braven reentered the lair and awoke Keyloi who stretched and rubbed his eyes and face.

"Oh, I am so sore." The boy rubbed his shoulders and neck.

"Yes, it was because we held the doors so tightly last night for so long. We probably need a different place to stay tonight. They know where we are and will be back."

Keyloi administered another dose of pain-killers to Braven. Braven appreciated the medicine but knew it was just a temporary fix for the real problem.

"There are only two more doses. These last twelve hours each, so after tomorrow you won't have any relief."

"They've been good for me, so I'll try to make them last longer."

"Not with you crawling through windows and fighting off caprodomes."

"You have a good point."

They gathered their goods to leave. Braven thought they should try to enter the air portal to see if there was any way to communicate. They would need to stay clear of the monolith and work around the debris.

As they approached the portal, they entered the perimeter and scouted the area. There was a monolith outside the air portal, but the structure was basically intact with no visible damage. The other monolith stood in place of the shuttle pad.

After surveying the scene, Braven said, "let's go see what we can find inside."

They pried the doors open. After they entered, Braven secured the doors. They saw what looked like a quick evacuation. Furniture was disheveled. Personal belongings still sat beside benches. They searched the abandoned personal effects but found no databoard.

They continued their search, opening doors throughout the structure—offices, storeroom, janitorial closet, breakroom, equipment room, relief station, conference room. Finally, a communications room.

They put their goods on a table, and Braven went to work to get a message to the space portal. He tried to initiate the equipment but had no luck.

"Power source. We need a power source." He searched the wall and floor panels to find a power source. Nothing. "I know they have backup power somewhere."

They scanned the room.

They rummaged through drawers and cabinets, opened equipment doors, and looked along walls, ceilings, and floors. Nothing.

"Why does this have to be so difficult?" Braven mumbled to himself.

"Do you think they took all the power blocks with them?"

"Probably. They were the last to leave and had time to plan. If we could just find a simple databoard."

They exited the next door which opened to the conference room. They did a thorough search but found nothing. Room after room, they hunted for their treasure.

They entered the breakroom and found some nourishment that was left. They sat at one of the tables and quietly enjoyed their meals.

"What if we don't find anything? Will we be here forever?"

After a short pause, Braven answered. "I'm not sure. I've never encountered an evacuation before now. I don't know if anyone returns to make sure everyone was evacuated or not."

"Don't they know we're missing and will come look for us?"

"Well, in my case, they probably thought I was killed when the monolith erupted. That's when I lost my databoard. When I awoke, I was covered with debris on top of a building. I was alone. In your case, I'm not sure."

Keyloi lowered his head. "I didn't tell you the truth."

"About what? Is your dad not a physician?"

"Oh, no, he is, but I stayed here on purpose. I wanted to be involved in the action and see a real caprodome. Everyone talks about them. I didn't want to stay with him. When I realized everyone was leaving, it was too late."

"What do you mean you didn't want to stay with him?"

"Oh, I was just mad at him. It's nothing."

They finished munching on their meals in silence. Braven tried to interact with no success. He glanced around the room, and up on a high shelf, there was a databoard. He quickly made his way over to the shelf. It was hidden under a towel with the corner exposed. He took it and tried to power it up. Nothing.

"It needs recharging. I'll put it in Capria's light for a little while." He hurried to a door which opened onto an eastern veranda. He placed the databoard so it could receive the most afternoon light.

The pair cheered.

"Now we need to wait for a charge, send a message, and then wait for someone to come get us."

As they stood outside, they heard a small squeak.

They both dropped to the ground.

"Get inside, quickly."

They reentered the building and heard it again as the door closed.

"It knows we're here," Keyloi whispered.

"Yes, it does. We need to keep it from exposing our location. Let's go get it and lock it in one of the rooms."

"Good idea."

They opened the door to find the little limya dancing around. It was so playful and enticing. Keyloi exited and played with it for a few seconds. He picked it up.

"Now, where do we put it?" he asked.

"We need to find a room where we will not be. They can probably hear his squeaks, so it needs to be a quiet room."

"What about the communications room? Aren't they usually soundproof?"

"You're just a sharp fellow today. Let's do it."

They carried the little critter to the room and went inside. There were no windows, it had insulated walls, and it was a perfect place to stash their tattletale.

They put the limya down and closed the door. The squeaking disappeared. They listened intently but could hear nothing.

"Perfect! Good job Keyloi. Now we need to find a shelter of our own."

They looked in the other rooms. Most had windows, only the equipment and janitor's rooms did not.

"I'm tired of sleeping in closets."

Braven chuckled. "We'll stay in the equipment room."

It was getting dusk. Braven got the databoard and went inside. He closed and locked all exterior doors. Keyloi and he entered the equipment room and settled in for the night.

Braven took the databoard and powered it up. He tried to send an N-Line message.

Rejected.

"What?" He tried again. Nothing.

He tried to send a message to his parents, Weston, the Scout headquarters, even Khara. Nothing.

"What's going on?"

He researched the system and discovered the communications port had been disabled. He enabled it and tried again.

His message to the Scout Center was sent. He sent one to his parents. Success. He messaged Weston. Same.

"Keyloi, what is your dad's contact?"

"I don't know."

"What's his name, and I can find him?"

"That's okay. I'll see him when we get there."

Braven paused. "Keyloi?"

"It's okay. I don't want to talk about it."

Braven hesitated to say anything.

"Well, I should be getting something from HQ or my parents soon. I already told them about you."

"Braven, it's okay." His voice was sullen. "He's not very nice to me."

"What do you mean? Does your dad abuse you?"

Keyloi closed his eyes and would not respond.

"Hey Keyloi, what's going on?"

"Nothing. It's okay."

"Keyloi, if you need to talk about something, I am your only listener."

"Maybe later." The youth looked up. Braven could see the hurt in his eyes.

"When you're ready to talk, I'm right here for you."

The pair sat quietly without speaking.

The databoard showed that Capria had set almost an hour earlier. Braven was happy to have the device.

What's up with Keyloi? He should be happy for the chance to leave here. What is this about his father? Do they not have a good relationship?

"Hey, why don't you go ahead and get some rest. Hopefully, we won't have any problems tonight."

Keyloi lay back and turned away from Braven.

This is the second night he has been upset with me.

The night trudged on. Braven heard no sounds

outside the room, but the night was just beginning.

He received an N-Line from HQ.

HQ: Braven! I can't believe you're alive. Reports were that you were caught in a monolith. Scout Zacor only found your databoard and power light. We will get to you soon.
Me: The shuttle pad was destroyed by a monolith. There are caprodomes everywhere all night. We will be safe tonight and will be awaiting rescue soon.

Braven knew he wouldn't receive their reply soon so he thought he would try to nap. He set the alarm to vibrate in one hour. He wanted to make sure all was good throughout the night, and they weren't surprised while sleeping.

The databoard vibrated his alarm. Braven opened his eyes. He listened for any noises, but there were none. He checked the databoard and found messages from HQ, his parents, and Weston.

HQ: If you can secure safe shelter tonight, a rescue flight has been planned for the morning. We will keep you updated as of the time.
Me: Looking forward to being with everyone and away from this planet.

Mom: I knew you would be okay. You never cease to amaze your dad and me with your survival skills. We love you and hope to see you soon.

Me: We are fine and looking forward to being with you two soon. Love you lots.

Weston: Braven! I'm so relieved you're alive. HQ is finalizing rescue plans. Chrysila is beautiful and wants to meet you. See you soon.

Me: So excited to leave this place. Looking forward to meeting her.

Braven leaned against the wall and smiled. He was relieved that he was able to find this databoard and send an N-Line. So many things could have gone wrong. The databoard could have been broken, unable to be charged, or have no communication link. He could have missed seeing it lying on the top shelf under the towel. Everything seemed to work together for their good.

He set the alarm for another hour and lay down. Silence. Peace. Pain. He had ignored the pain in his side that seemed to grow as the day progressed. He wanted to wait until the morning before receiving another dose so he could have a reserve before leaving the planet.

As he lay quietly, he could hear faint noises. He felt safe that the creatures weren't close to them. The sense of security and quiet peacefulness lured him into a restful sleep.

Vibrations from the databoard woke him. It was dark and quiet. No sense of worry. He reset for another hour and fell back to sleep.

The databoard shook under his arm. He opened his eyes. All was at peace. He reset it for another hour.

He opened his eyes to more vibrations. All was quiet. He faced the databoard light toward Keyloi who was fast asleep. He reset the alarm and rested.

After a few more times, he noticed that Capria would rise within the hour. He sat up and leaned against the wall. All was still quiet.

He checked his N-Line. One response from HQ.

HQ: Rescue scheduled for 1000. Meet north of the air portal.

Me: Acknowledged. Two passengers.

Braven was elated. He waited until just before Capria rose to awaken Keyloi.

"What time is it?"

"Capria is just now rising, and I have good news. Rescue will be here in four hours."

"Wonderful." He turned his head back to the wall; there was no excitement in his voice.

Braven hesitated but then decided to probe. "Keyloi, what's wrong? You act as if you don't want to be rescued."

A short pause. The youth sat up and leaned against the wall. "It's not that I don't want to be rescued. It's just that I don't have much to look forward to when I return."

"What about your parents?"

"I have no parents."

"Your dad, the physician?"

"He's not my dad. My parents were killed in a landslide accident at home on Radzier. I didn't want to be reminded of them, so I wanted to leave the planet. I met up with the physician who lost his family in the same accident. Soon afterwards, he was assigned here, so he brought me with him."

"Did he adopt you?"

"No, he got someone to make up papers."

"Oh, Keyloi. That's illegal."

"I know it. I gave him my inheritance from my parents to bring me with him. He's a bully, and I don't want to live with him anymore."

"That's a lot for a twelve-year-old to handle. When we return, I'll see what I can do for you. How about that?"

The boy's eyes widened, and his countenance changed. "Will you do that?"

"Of course. I don't know what all can be done, but I'll investigate it."

"Thank you! I'll repay you somehow."

"You're welcome, and you can repay me with another dose."

Braven could see a change in his demeanor. He looked forward to helping this young friend of his. A dose was administered, and Braven found quick relief.

"How did you get to be so brave?" Keyloi asked.

"Oh," Braven paused, "I've not always been brave. It's just something I've learned about how to react to situations."

"Will you teach me? You think I could be a Scout when I get older?"

Braven smiled. "I know you can, and I'd be happy to teach you."

The boy smiled. Braven was honored. He felt like he had become Weston, and Keyloi was his younger self.

He looked at the time and realized Capria should have already risen. Braven slowly opened the door to peer outside. Light flooded their room.

Braven felt exhilarated. It was daytime, rescue was coming, and his pain subsided. "Another night down. Hopefully the last."

They stepped outside the room into the air portal's central room. Everything was the same as the night before.

"The caps didn't come here last night."

"Yeah, the limya couldn't go report where we were."

They chuckled.

"Speaking of the limya," Braven stated, "we need to let it out. We should not be cruel and allow it to starve to death."

Braven went to open the door. As soon as the door was opened, the limya ran out and loudly squealed at them both. The sound was not the pleasing squeak they had heard earlier. It ran to the exterior door, back to them making the same harsh noise, and then back to the exterior door.

"I think it's angry at us. Open the door so it can leave."

Keyloi opened the door, the limya shot outside toward the colony as fast as it could and made that obnoxious noise as it sped away.

Braven and Keyloi stood in awe.

"What was that all about?"

Braven was bumfuzzled. "That was strange." He shook his head in a negative reply.

"We have four hours before the rescue is planned. And it will be just outside to the north. Until then, we just need to wait."

"Four long hours." Keyloi stressed.

"Yep. Four long, boring hours. Nothing to do. No one to visit. No caprodomes to torment us. What can happen in four hours? Maybe we should take a nap."

Keyloi snapped his head toward his senior. "I'm not taking a nap this time. I'm ready to leave."

Both laughed aloud.

Section 14

Overcome

Braven looked around the landscape. He didn't think he would miss the flat, cyan-covered land. He wondered where he would be assigned. Maybe he will have some adventures next time.

The two exchanged comments about the surroundings and their time at Alpha. Keyloi had only been on planet for two years.

Two years. Braven compared that to the fifteen years he had been there. *So many other worlds to explore.*

The two returned inside for some nourishment. They savored their breakfast. Braven checked for messages. There were none. He looked at the time—three hours to rescue.

"What do you want to do for three hours?"

Keyloi hesitated. "Stay right here."

Braven chuckled. That was good for him.

About an hour later, they felt a movement.

"Groundquake?" Keyloi's eyes widened.

"Yes." Braven looked concerned. His senses were heightened to anything unusual.

After a few minutes, they relaxed. It may have been closer to the colony.

In the faint distance, Braven heard familiar squeals. He peered out the large, scenic window. There, bouncing on all fours at the base of the portal structure, was the limya.

"The limya is back."

"You're joking! It doesn't take hints very well."

Braven watched it bounce in one place. It ran to his left and did the same, and then continued around the building. Every five meters, it would stop and bounce.

Why is it doing that? Is it trying to get our attention?

Braven moved to the door and went outside. Nothing was around but the tiny creature. He walked out onto the veranda and watched the animal do its bouncing act. Keyloi joined him outside.

"What is it doing? Why is it squealing like it did this morning when we let it out."

The creature continued its act, completely circling the building. Carefully, Braven walked to the edge of the limya's circle. As the creature neared them, it expanded its circle five meters and continued its dance around the structure.

Something doesn't seem right.

"Keyloi, we need to move."

Braven grabbed the boy's arm and began running from the limya away from the building. Suddenly, the ground exploded under the air portal. The males, as well as the structure, were sent skyward. Braven landed hard on his back. Parts of the structure landed on top of him. Severe pain shot through his body. He held his screams but openly moaned.

Dirt and debris covered the once-serene scene. Thick dust hung in the air. It was difficult to breathe. Braven pulled his shirt over his mouth. He coughed. Pain.

"Keyloi?"

No answer. Braven coughed. He groaned. Pain swirled in his body. A part of the building material pierced his left thigh and blood gushed out.

"Keyloi."

Braven could hear coughing. He knew Keyloi was still alive.

He pushed debris off his body and assessed himself. The protruding shard caused excruciating agony more than the broken ribs. Braven yelled out in distress. He knew he shouldn't remove the fragment, but he couldn't walk with it sticking out of his leg. He grabbed the intruding object and yanked it out of his leg. He screamed. He removed his shirt and wound it tightly around his thigh to try and stop the exiting blood.

"Keyloi!"

The dust slowly settled. The air portal was gone, and an enormous monolith stood in its place. Most of the building had been displaced to Braven's left side. Fortunately, Keyloi was thrown to Braven's right side during the eruption.

Braven again called for the youth.

"Here." Keyloi gagged and coughed.

Braven looked through the residual dust but could not locate him.

He coughed again.

Braven looked in that direction and saw some movement. He struggled to get up. With the injuries, his pain was overwhelming. He managed to move toward his companion and found him covered in debris.

"Keyloi!"

"I'm...here."

"Are you injured?"

"My head hurts. I think it's bleeding. And my hand."

Braven struggled to make his way around to the youth.

"Let's get clear of this and move away from here."

They cleared the debris so Keyloi could stand. Blood streamed down his right cheek. He was holding his left hand. Braven quickly examined him to find a gash behind his ear. His hand was possibly broken. He told him to hold his other hand over the cut to help stop the bleeding.

The two helped each other and slowly moved away from the scene of destruction. The rescue would be north of the air portal, so that was where they headed.

Upon moving many meters away, they turned and surveyed the scene of the once-useful building. A huge monolith stood in its place. It was only ten meters tall but twice the size of the other structures' circumference.

"How did you know when to run?"

Braven thought of the question. He had seen the limya's unusual behavior and used his instincts.

"The limya was acting oddly. I felt we needed to get away from it."

"The limya? What does that have to do with a monolith?"

"The limya worked with the caprodomes. Remember the night it ran away from us? It returned and made the coaxing squeak to get us out of our shelter while the caprodomes were waiting for us. The caprodomes work with the monoliths to bring it food. So, I figure all three creatures work together for survival."

"Oh, I see." Keyloi was in thought. "So, when the limya was back and dancing around and squealing really loud, it was alerting the monolith?"

"I can't see it any other way. It's a symbiotic relationship between the three."

"How strange."

"We're on a different planet full of unusual creations. We must not rule out anything, no matter how bizarre."

The limya came around the corner of the debris and peered at the two. Its piercing squeal was unbearable. It ran around the pair and began its dance once again.

"Oh, no you don't." Braven picked up a piece of debris and threw it at the little creature. Keyloi joined in the barrage. The limya ran behind the monolith still squealing.

"We need to get away from that thing. Who knows what it will do."

They moved away from the little creature who followed them. Wherever they went, the critter was right behind, making its absurd squealing noise.

"Can we lock that thing inside somewhere so it will leave us alone?"

"It's not going to let us get close enough to catch it."

Keyloi threw a piece of debris at it, and it hit the animal in the rump. The limya yipped and ran toward the colony, squealing as it went. The two watched the creature as it disappeared among the buildings.

"You took care of that. Good throw."

Keyloi displayed a look of success.

Braven looked at the boy's injured head. It was superficial, and the bleeding had slowed. Keyloi complained of a headache. His hand had begun to swell. It definitely looked like it was broken.

They found some large rocks about fifty meters north of the air portal to rest on and wait for their rescue. They did not want to return to the colony or any of the creatures.

Braven removed the blood-soaked shirt to check his leg, but it was still steadily oozing, so he retightened it.

He assumed two hours passed. He left the databoard inside the building. They could only surmise the time and how long it would be until help arrived.

Braven was glad he received the dologra before the monolith arrived. The puncture in his leg, matched with the pain in his chest, was bad enough with the painkillers. He could not imagine being without the medicine.

They exchanged small talk until they noticed the limya returning toward them at full speed.

"What now?" Keyloi picked up a fist-sized rock and readied it.

The squealing grew, but this time, it echoed from the colony. The two spied a small group of the creatures followed. At least six limyas were running and making the same noise.

The two males stood not knowing what to do. There was no shelter nearby, and Braven could not outrun them with his injuries. He quickly got his stun pistol. Keyloi grabbed rocks. They were poised for an attack.

The limyas surrounded the two and again conducted their high-pitched noises and dances. They all bounced in sequence.

Keyloi threw rocks. Braven grabbed the few rocks near him and hurled them at the attackers. As the two moved in one direction, the beasts followed them. They all remained in circumference and perfect uniform as if they knew what the other would do.

"We need to get away from these things. Just start moving that way." Braven pointed as he yelled his orders. "They are alerting the monolith of where we are."

The two moved to the north, and the limyas moved along with them. They shifted east, and the creatures followed.

They found more rocks and quickly flung them toward their assailants. Braven ignited his pistol toward them, but the flare only leaped twenty-five centimeters. They continued relocating so there was no stationary position for a large attack.

Many minutes lapsed and the creatures would not surrender their harassment. Braven and Keyloi felt a small groundquake and quickly made their way farther north. It stopped. The incessant shrieking reverberated through their heads.

They continued heading north and westward in random ways and did not stop. The pain in Braven's leg exploded as he needed to rest, but he knew the consequences. He continued through the agony.

The limyas continued their madness. The humanoids continued their defense.

Wind and dust blew over the scene. Braven knew they were history and expected to be catapulted into the air. Maybe into the mouth of the monolith. The limyas grew louder.

One limya fell over as if dead. Another repeated, then another, as if they were being hit by something. A groundquake stirred. Something grabbed Braven from behind and began pulling him. He yelled. The ground exploded.

***

Braven was lifted into a hilo. Keyloi sat with him. They went airborne. Braven glanced at the ground to see a new monolith surrounded by clouds of dust and two limyas running about. He looked around the hilo at five military personnel.

"Scout Triton?"

"Yes, ma'am, and this is Keyloi Gravton. Thank you for coming."

"Of course, our pleasure," the young female said with a grin.

They were taken kilometers away toward the north to an air shuttle resting on a solid location. The hilo landed, the passengers were unloaded, and the aircraft collapsed and was loaded into the shuttle. Braven was amazed as he had never seen that happen.

***

The welcoming party was exuberant. Braven's parents, Weston and his family, Khara, and the entire squad of Scouts were present. No one arrived to greet Keyloi. Braven's heart hurt for the youth. He kept the youth close to him.

The two were taken to the medical unit for assessment. Braven had three broken ribs and a deep laceration and puncture in his thigh which barely missed his femoral artery. Keyloi had a slight concussion, two broken fingers, and numerous cuts. They were treated and released over the next few days.

Braven investigated Keyloi's situation. The boy's parents and the physician's family were all killed during the Radzierian accident as Keyloi had explained. The physician relented to his illegal activities and was sent away for internment.

Braven, along with his parents, asked Keyloi if he would join their family. Adoptions in the colonies were quickly completed due to the fragility and support of life. That was no exception in Keyloi's case. He became Keyloi Triton, part of the Triton family, and brother to the man he most admired.

Check out the other books in The Journeys of Braven Series and this author.

The Jediran Quest, Book 1

The Mines of Jedira, Book 2

ABOUT THE AUTHOR

Cal Davis created and wrote stories when he was a teenager. He just didn't like reading at school, because there was always an exam. Reading should be for fun, right? After college (and a lot of reading!), he enjoyed a couple of overseas tours in the Air Force and ended up teaching middle school. A few years later, he took a position in the housing industry, working on 30-years for retirement.

Cal loves writing and telling stories with purpose for children. He wrote the picture books "I'm Just a Crow" and "Look, Look, Look What I Did!" to show children to be the person they were created to be and not cave to peer pressure. His award-winning books, "The Jediran Quest" and "The Mines of Jedira," of the *Journeys of Braven Series* gives examples of leadership and character-building for young teens. Many of his books grant Accelerated Reading (AR) points for primary and middle schoolers. He enjoys helping other authors in their pursuit of the literary world and still believes *Reading should be fun!*

Email: caldavisauthor@gmail.com

Website: www.caldavisauthor.com

Facebook: www.facebook.com/caldavisauthor

www.ingramcontent.com/pod-product-compliance
Lightning Source LLC
Chambersburg PA
CBHW051955220626
47052CB00004B/958

* 9 7 8 1 9 6 2 3 1 8 0 2 0 *